WOLF MOON

GIFTS FROM THE GODDESS: BOOK 1

MIRANDA HARVEY &
CATE ALEXANDER

Whoever said diamonds were a girl's best friend never had a dog ...

For Bronson – May you run forever free over the rainbow bridge

— M.H.

For my Alice-Puppy. There may be a reason my daughters think you're my favourite child

— C.A

CHAPTER 1

As she crouched in the fallen autumn leaves, their browns and ambers working to camouflage the copper tinge in her fur, she watched the people below through the trees. Her right hind leg twitched from lying in the same position since dawn, but she ignored it. After a week of living in the national park, she needed a shower, a hot meal, and to remember what it felt like to be human. Though only early Fall the weather had already started to turn cold, and she didn't want to spend another winter shivering in her wolf body, especially considering how lean she was at the moment, in every form. She needed to find somewhere to lay low for the next few months.

At her last stop, she had popped into an internet café to search the local area. The results revealed that the coming months would be quieter here in Peregrine now the famous cherry season had ended. Tourists would have had their fill of cherries and headed home, leaving the locals to enjoy their town. It was always a challenge, finding places that weren't brimming with people but still had enough jobs, cash jobs, available to strangers passing through.

"Just call me a modern-day gypsy," she thought to herself with a wry grin.

Sniffing the air, she picked up hints of coffee and bacon wafting from the cafes serving breakfast on the main street. Hearing her stomach rumble, she let it decide for her. Her wolf self might be happy with just the bacon, but her human self was craving coffee. She would check out the town and, if it wasn't suitable, leave to find another. She still had time before the snow started. Turning, the wolf wove between the trees to the place she had hidden her backpack. While she was grateful that her clothes remained when she changed, it frustrated her that essentials, like her purse and watch, did not. Sitting down, her back to the tree to hide her, she started to think herself human. She knew this change wouldn't be easy. The longer she spent in another form, the longer it took to change back. Sometimes she wondered if a time would come when she would forget that she was human. Closing her eyes, slowing her breathing, so it was regular, deep, and calm, she thought about her family. Her parents, her brother Matthew and her sister Emily would probably still be in bed, enjoying the sleep-in the weekend provided. Thinking of them was always bittersweet, filling her with an intense longing. Not knowing when, or if, she would see them again felt like a raw wound that never healed. Next, she thought about the things she would have to give up if she stayed in wolf form. It wasn't a long list, and it kept getting shorter every time she had to move to another place, but there were still things she loved. A wolf couldn't drink coffee, or read a book, or enjoy the first sip of a cold beer on a hot day. With each thing she remembered, she felt her body relax, and the magic at her core start to flow. She imagined it as a well of golden light which flowed from her heart to her finger-tips, her toes, and her brow. When she opened her eyes, she was human once more.

Standing, she brushed dirt and leaves off her jeans and sweatshirt and pulled a twig out of her long red hair. Ugh. She loved her waist-length hair, and the warmth a shaggy coat provided when she was a wolf, but twigs and leaves were a hazard to her hair in both forms. She had left the last town in a hurry, and one of the pants legs sported a ripped knee. Another reason to return to civilization. For the moment though they would have to do. Pushing aside the cover of leaves, she picked up her small backpack and slung it over her shoulder. There was no need to check the contents; she knew them by heart. The bare essentials. Wolf-people traveled light. Making her way carefully down the steep hill she headed towards the town, following the scent of coffee.

Bacon, eggs, and a velvety latte from the Black Market coffee shop eased her hunger pains. As she picked up a folded map from the counter stand, a smiling waitress, recognizing her as a tourist, asked if she was staying at the Hotel Sienna. Caley shook her head. The expensive-look-ing, eight-story hotel was far outside her price range. Her wallet, after she paid for the delicious breakfast, held a little over $200, the last of her savings from her previous stint of life in civilization. After explaining to the smiling girl that she was backpacking, the waitress suggested she try The Last Drop. They had rooms above the bar which they rented at a reasonable price during the slow season. Caley thanked her for her kindness. Her travels had taught her that you could often judge a town by how the staff treated strangers and, so far, this place was looking pretty good.

Deciding that a shower was next on her list of priorities, Caley started in the direction of the bar. Her eyes took in sidelong glances of the people enjoying the clear morning air. The many bicycles almost outnumbered the cars, and the main street was surprisingly busy for that time of day. Caley tried to avoid looking too long at the shocking amounts of bright spandex. Readjusting to the flow of a town was something that might take some getting used to, but she loved the idea of a community that lived outdoors, Lycra notwithstanding. Families with small children gathered in the cafes chatting and enjoying a lazy morning. She saw several people had dogs lying at their feet, lapping water from provided bowls. A wave of relief flooded over her, another good sign. She took careful note of the various breeds. This information could come in handy; hopefully, another dog wandering the town wouldn't draw too much unwanted attention.

Reaching The Last Drop, half a dozen streets back from the main road, she discovered it to be a four-story, brownstone, turn-of-the-century building. One of the downstairs windows had been blocked out with black-board paint. Handwritten words in white chalk promoted the days' specials. The bar also served food, offering breakfast, lunch, and dinner, and there would be a live band playing that night. A sign hanging above the entrance proclaimed that they had a vacancy. Pushing open the heavy doors, Caley was relieved not to be assaulted by the smell of cigarettes and stale beer. The ground floor of the bar was neat and tidy, with wooden floorboards instead of carpet and fans spinning from the rafters to clear the air. A drum kit and a pair of microphones adorned the stage in the far corner edged by a dance floor. Tables and stools were scattered around, inviting patrons to sit and watch. It gave a relaxed air. Caley liked it. Behind those small tables, closer to the bar, larger tables were arranged in a more orderly fashion, decorated with ketchup and mustard bottles, napkins, and salt and pepper shakers. Between the sets of tables were two green felted pool tables acting as a barrier between bar and restaurant.

A woman, long dark hair piled on top of her head in a messy bun, stood behind the bar cleaning glasses. A pair of glasses hung from a chain around her neck, jiggling against her ample bosom with the twisting movement of the cleaning cloth. As Caley stepped closer to the bar the woman called out, "Morning love, how can I help you?" her voice warm and friendly.

Caley smiled back. "I saw your vacancy sign. I was wondering how much you charge for a room?"

As the woman's gaze scanned her, Caley felt her cheeks flush with heat due to the dirty state of her clothes. Perhaps she should have gone clothes shopping first, but a roof over her head had been her priority, well that and the lure of a long, hot shower. As if sensing her discomfort, the woman smiled.

"You traveling by yourself? It's a bit late in the year for backpackers. You missed a hell of a cherry season. If you aren't fussy about your room, I've got a double on the third floor that you can have cheap. I'll even throw in a free dinner with the room."

Caley self-consciously wrapped her arms around her waist, aware that she had lost weight and must look like a wraith. In wolf form, she had no choice but to eat her food raw, and she hadn't been able to bring herself to hunt most evenings.

"Ahh love, I didn't mean to embarrass you or make you feel awkward," the woman said, "It's my Italian upbringing. My husband Frank figures that I'd adopt the world if I could."

"That's okay. How much is the room?"

"$65 a night."

Caley did a quick calculation in her head. Her $200 would stretch to 3 nights but leave no change for clothes or other essentials. Hopefully, she would be able to pick up a job quickly, otherwise, she would be back to sleeping in the woods again.

"I'd like to stay for two, please."

"Alright. I'm Melody, but you can call me Mel," the woman held out her hand, its palm calloused from years of hard work. Caley shook it. It was strange to feel the touch of another person.

"I'm Caley."

. . .

The room Melody had shown her was small, the ceiling slanted following the line of the roof, and was furnished only with two single beds, each pushed against a side wall, with a small bed-side table and a lamp a piece. Despite this, it had a cozy feel. A hand-knitted pink and blue blanket added a splash of color to the white walls, and a cotton rug took the chill from the floor. Melody offered to push the beds together, but Caley told her not to bother. All the guests shared the bathroom, but Melody had promised the hot water flowed freely, it was on gas so it wouldn't run out. It felt blissful after so many days of bathing in Lake Michigan.

Promising to be back in time for dinner, Caley headed to the local mall purchasing a new pair of jeans and a couple of sweatshirts from Wallmart. With one of her few, precious last dollars, she also bought a postcard, stamp, and a copy of the local newspaper. Borrowing a pen from the woman behind the counter, Caley sat on a bench outside the mall. When she had left home, escaping those that hunted her, she had made a promise to her mom always to let them know where she was. It was a promise she had no intention of breaking.

Arrived safely. People here are nice. Hope to stay a while. Wish you were here. Miss you all.

Like all her postcards she didn't address it to anyone, and she didn't sign it. The words were simple, nothing that could be traced or reveal who the sender was. Despite this, to keep her safe, her mom would likely burn it once they'd read it. Sighing, she posted it in the old-fashioned blue mailbox and went back into the mall to return the borrowed pen. Shopping bag in hand, she made her way slowly back to the bar, but instead of heading inside, she slipped around the back of the building. From the high window in her room, she had looked down and seen the dumpster, hidden from patron view behind a metal gate. Opening it, wincing at the sound of creaking metal, she snuck inside the barrier. Undoing her watch and slipping it inside her backpack, she swapped it for the tagged dog collar, then put the backpack into the plastic bag holding her new clothes. She shoved the bag under the dumpster, hoping that the horrible smell wouldn't invade its contents through the plastic.

Crouching, she closed her eyes and calmed her breathing. She focused her thoughts on the golden Labrador she'd seen a little girl feeding pieces of her bagel to that morning. The change was straightforward, and Caley felt the magic flow through her, like a warm caress. Opening her eyes, she looked out, sniffing the air. The dumpster which had smelt foul to her human nose now smelt interesting. For half a moment she thought about diving in, looking for the tempting food scraps, but then remembered she would have a proper meal for dinner that night. Slipping her head through the elasticized collar, she pushed open the metal gate and ran out into the afternoon to explore her new home.

CHAPTER 2

Caley sighed contentedly as she laid down her knife and fork. The meal of steak, mashed potatoes, carrots and peas, all covered in a rich gravy, had chased away her hunger pangs entirely. Running around the town on four paws, not to mention changing form three times in a day, had left her famished. The run had done her good, clearing her mind and putting her in a happier mood. She now felt adequately human. The thought made her grin as she reached across her empty plate to pick up the newspaper. She had just started scouring the job section when her attention was caught by the ringing of the bell above the entry door. Glancing up over the top of the paper, she saw a couple enter the bar. A dark-haired, bearded man with a giggling woman clinging to his arm like a barnacle. They looked as if this bar wasn't their first stop for the night. Behind them, keeping a slight distance between them, was a clean-shaven blond man. His eyes roamed the bar, taking in the handful of patrons and the performers. Caley had the feeling that nothing would escape this man's notice, his gaze making the hairs on the back of her neck prickle.

"Owen, Mike, good to see you fellas here tonight. The usual?" Mel called out from behind the bar and Caley instantly relaxed. Regulars. Nothing to worry about. Ignoring the rest of their conversation, she went back to scanning the paper for work. A couple of the wineries were looking for help picking the late harvest of grapes. One of the cafes was advertising for an experienced barista. She circled both. She was partway through circling a job for a dishwasher at a local restaurant when a loud crack made her jump. Startled, the red pen she'd been using streaked the page as her hand flew up. Looking around, terrified, her wide eyes took in the tipsy couple and the blond-haired man, standing around one of the pool tables. The sound which had startled her turned out to be nothing more than the crack of the white ball against the colors, starting their game.

"Sorry, didn't mean to scare you." Looking up Caley saw it was the blond guy she'd watched enter earlier. It must be Owen or Mike. Mmm. If she were the betting type, she'd guess Owen. Mostly because the bearded guy looked so much like a Mike. He had a kind, open face with the faint lines around his mouth, showing him as the sort of man who smiled a lot. He was smiling now. An apologetic smile, yet also friendly. The white, collared t-shirt he wore tucked into his dark blue jeans displayed arms which showed off his now much-faded summer tan. She guessed he worked a job which kept him outside during the summer. He looked nice, but Caley had been fooled by nice before.

"No bother," she said, breaking eye contact before it had a chance to evolve. She felt him move away, an absence of warmth and presence in the air and went back to browsing the job advertisements. Try as she might, however, she couldn't seem to focus on the printed words. Creasing her brow in concentration, she tried to ignore the sounds of laughter and banter coming from the three friends around the pool table. The dark-haired man kept complaining that his blond friend was winning. After what Caley guessed to be three rounds, the blond man let his friend and the girl play alone while he went to the bar to get drinks. This provided Caley with a further distraction as she couldn't help peering at the firm curve of his butt in the well-fitting jeans as he walked towards the bar. Catching Mel's eye, whose smirk proved that she was caught in the act, Caley looked down again quickly, using the newspaper to hide her flush.

She was trying to focus on an advert for aisle stockers at the local grocery store when she heard a cough. Looking up, she was not surprised to see the blond man with the cute butt.

"I was wondering if you would mind doing me a favor?" he asked. His tone was straight forward, with no leer or presumption that men often approached her with, but still, she was hesitant.

"What sort of favor?"

Her doubt must have shown in her voice because he quickly shook his head.

"Oh no! Nothing like that." She could have sworn his cheeks reddened and, sympathetically, she smiled openly at him. His smile of relief matched her own. Putting down the three pints of beer, he held one hand out to her. "I'm Owen."

"Caley," she said, almost slipping up and giving him her full name. There was something so honest and friendly about this guy that she struggled to deceive him. She was also oddly pleased to find she'd been right about his name.

"That is Mike," he pointed to the dark-haired man, "And his girlfriend Lisa." Noticing her attention, the two waved, then went back to flirting over a cue and felted table. "As you can see, I am clearly the third wheel. When those two get all lovey-dovey, I miss having someone to talk to." Again, the words were friendly instead of suggestive. "I saw you sitting alone and thought it might be a good opportunity to have someone to talk to, maybe make a new friend." He smiled, showing off a dimple in the right cheek she hadn't noticed before. Later, Caley wouldn't be sure if it was the dimple or being alone in the woods for so long that made her nod her head in agreement. Whatever it was, her policy of going unnoticed didn't get a second thought in that instance.

Owen introduced her to his friends who instantly gave up their game, which they hadn't been making much effort with anyway, and Mike started to collect the balls and rack up for a fresh set.

"Can I get you a drink?" Owen asked. Caley paused before answering. She would love a cold beer, but her meager funds wouldn't support buying another round. Again, Owen seemed to read her mind. "On me. As a thank you for doing me this favor."

Caley smiled, "I would love a Fosters, please."

"Done."

Watching Owen walk to the bar, she smiled. Maybe this town was going to work out just fine. Perhaps she could even make some new friends. Giving Caley a welcoming smile and the brunette a kiss on the cheek, Mike followed Owen to the bar giving the girls a chance to get to know each other.

"He's cute, isn't he?" the girl, Lisa, asked with a nudge.

Not wanting her to get the wrong idea, Caley replied, "He seems nice." Before Lisa could ask another awkward question, she said, "You and Mike look like a cute couple." Lisa immediately launched into the story of how she met Mike, how long they had been together, and how she was hoping he was going to ask her to move in with him soon. Caley had quickly learned that if she wanted to avoid personal questions she struggled to answer, the simplest solution was usually to reflect attention back on the person asking the questions. Most people enjoyed talking about themselves.

Lisa was just asking Caley where she was staying and how long she intended to be in town when the two men returned with the drinks providing a convenient distraction. Thanking Owen, Caley accepted the beer and took a large swallow. The cold liquid soothed her anxiety as she quickly tried to put together a backstory. In the past, her role was a backpacker passing through, a tourist from Canada and even a travel writer. Previously she had managed to get by with just necessary details. She had actively avoided getting too close to anyone, but since she was hoping to stay here a little longer, she knew she would have to come up with something less auspicious. She had planned to work on her story that night alone in her room, but it seemed that circumstances had changed. Her right pinky finger started to twitch as she nervously tried to come up with a suitable reason for staying. Thinking it more straightforward to just make her escape, she was about to claim the onset of a sudden headache. Her thoughts were stalled, and she started to relax again when she realized that Lisa, distracted by the return of the men, had started up a game of pool. Her questions, for the moment at least, appeared to be forgotten.

Lisa grabbed the two pool cues off the stand as Mike started to rack up the balls, asking as he did so, "Are we playing ladies versus gents, or should we do couples?"

"I haven't played for a while, so I am kind of rusty," Caley admitted. She hadn't played in years, not since an almost forgotten holiday from before her world had turned upside down. Caley frowned as a rush of home-sickness washed over her. It had been a long time since she had done anything as ordinary as play a game of pool.

Misinterpreting her sadness as embarrassment, Mike said with a slight laugh, "Don't worry, you can't be worse than Lisa," which earned him a slap on the arm from the offended girl. That only made Mike laugh harder. "You know it's true. Pool has never been your strong point, too busy being distracted by my manliness." He struck a body builder pose. This got a laugh out of Lisa who kissed him passionately before challenging,

"Bring it on! Boys versus girls it is. Ladies first, so I'll break."

The game should have ended quickly with the girls, who were significantly outmatched by the men, losing by a landslide. But Lisa was using every trick in the book to distract Mike and put him off his game. Caley and Owen found themselves doubled over with laughter watching her harass Mike, who reveled in the attention. Caley found herself admiring Mike's focus, that he could hit the ball perfectly even while a pool cue was being run sensuously up and down the inside of his leg. Two beers down and she was feeling tipsy, the tension which had built up over the past weeks in the woods beginning to release. She couldn't remember the last time she laughed so hard.

As Mike leaned across the table, aiming for the black ball, which would win them the game, Lisa started to run her hands down the sides of his back.

"Time to use my secret weapon, Mr. Ticklish," Lisa teased.

Caley could see the muscles in Mike's back tense as he valiantly ignored the attack. Biting his lip, Mike's steely eyes remained focused on the ball. Owen, who when he wasn't playing always found his way to Caley's side, leaned towards her and said quietly with a wink, "She should know better than to try distracting a police officer. We are trained to deal with bigger threats than Lisa." As he looked at Caley with a warm grin, she felt an ice-cold shiver of fear run down her spine.

CHAPTER 3

A few hours later, Caley lay wide awake, staring at the slanted ceiling. After Owen's startling revelation that he and Mike were both police officers, she had become flustered and made a hurried excuse to leave. It was just her luck that the first friends she made in Peregrine City were the exact kinds of people she was trying to avoid. So much for flying under the radar. Owen had looked disappointed when she claimed a sudden migraine and left. Even Mel, busy pouring beers behind the bar, looked worried at her hasty exit. She had sprinted straight up to her room and gone to bed, freaking out about what to do next. Struggling to fall asleep, Caley battled with the idea of just packing her bags and disappearing. There were supplies she needed, but she could buy them in the morning and be gone before the sunset. Leaving the next day, Caley might find another place to stay before the freezing cold winter came. She couldn't face another winter in the woods.

Tossing and turning Caley eventually fell into a troubled sleep.

A hot shower usually worked to calm her nerves, but that morning, it had no effect. She couldn't stop the trembling in her hands, and it took her three attempts to do up the button on her jeans. Grabbing her purse, she headed down the stairs but froze a few steps from the bottom landing. Standing by the bar, as if waiting for her, was Owen. There was no denying the fact of his job now as she took in his pale blue uniform. If she weren't so scared, she would probably have taken the time to admire how well the color suited him and how the tight fit of his navy-blue pants outlined his muscular form. Taking a step backward, hoping to retreat without being seen, she instead caught her foot on the stair. The action caused her to lose her balance, and she fell hard on her butt. Instead of escaping silently, the jarring pain caused her to yelp. Within seconds Owen was in front of her, holding out his hand to help her up.

"Are you alright?" he asked, his voice full of concern. Caley felt blood rush to her cheeks in embarrassment, and for a moment, she was speechless. He saved her from having to answer by taking her hand and pulling her to a standing position. Looking up into his dark brown eyes, she felt another flush. Her hand in his large, rough, warm one was trembling, and he didn't let go. "I thought I would come by and check on you. You had me worried after you disappeared so quickly last night. I hope we didn't do anything to offend you?"

A little voice inside her head said that she should rebuff his attention with a rude word so that he would leave her alone, but there was something so open and honest in his concern that she instead found herself saying, "I'm sorry it was nothing to do with you or your friends. I think I was just tired from traveling."

"You poor thing. You were just trying to have a quiet night, and then we came and trampled it. I'm sorry," he said contritely.

"Don't be," she said, finding that she meant it. The pool game had been the most fun she'd had in ages, and she would remember it, keep it stored away like so many other precious memories to get her through lonely days in the woods. For a moment they both stood there awkwardly, neither one quite knowing what to say next. Owen still held her hand, but she didn't want to pull away. Her inner voice of caution was screaming at her, but the warning was drowned out by her heartbeat thumping loudly, echoing through her head. She was so tired of running.

The silence could have gone on for minutes or hours, Caley couldn't tell, but they both started when Mel's voice interrupted them. "Morning Caley. How did you sleep last night?"

Turning to Mel, Caley smiled, "Well, thank you." Even though worry had kept her awake for most of it, it was still the best sleep she'd had in months. She'd forgotten how good it felt sleeping in a soft bed under a blanket, with an actual pillow rather than a pile of leaves. Caley saw Mel notice her hand still held in Owen's and the barmaid gave her a broad grin. Embarrassed, Caley quickly pulled her hand out of his grasp.

"How about some breakfast?" Mel inquired. Caley felt

her stomach rumble in response, but she shook her head reluctantly. Her minuscule funds would barely cover the supplies Caley needed. It would seem she was in for another hungry day. Hopefully later, if a safe opportunity arose to shift, a hunting trip would be possible. She could catch fish in Lake Michigan if she could find a place where she wouldn't risk an icy bath. Raw fish was definitely preferable to raw meat. Even before her first change, she had been a fan of sashimi.

"So, what are you planning to do with your day?" Owen asked.

Without thinking of her plan to leave, she replied, "I need to find a job."

"What sort of work are you looking for?" Mel asked

"I'm not really sure. Something casual as I'm not sure how long I'll be staying. Maybe waitressing or something at the local supermarket."

"Do you have any experience working behind a bar? David, one of my regulars, is about to leave me for three months to go see his family and I could use the help. The pay isn't much, but it does include breakfast, and I can give you a further discount on your room if you're interested."

"Are you sure I wouldn't be putting you out? I can't promise that I'll be here for the full three months. You might be better off hiring someone who can commit."

"I'm sure. If you take the job now, it saves me the cost of advertising in the local paper. If you don't stay here for 3 months, then I'm no worse off than I would be now."

Caley hesitated for only a moment before nodding her head. "I'd love to work here. Thank you, Mel."

"Great! You can start tonight, and your first breakfast is on me. I'll get the cook to put something together for you now, and you can fill in the paperwork while you eat." Caley felt her finger twitch at the mention of the word paperwork. Her preference was finding cash-in-hand work off the books and thus avoiding leaving a record of her travels. But the opportunity for not only employment but included food and board was a temptation she couldn't resist. It meant, however, that her fake ID would be put to the test. Felix was a master of forgery, but it still made her nervous every time she used it.

"My shift is only a half-day today, I finish at noon. Since your day has cleared up, how about I show you around the town a bit later?" Owen offered. Caley surprised herself with her quick, "Yes, I'd like that." The warm smile he gave her in response was quickly matched by one of her own.

A few hours later, her belly full of bacon and eggs, and the completed paperwork and fake ID handed over, Caley met Owen outside the front of The Last Drop. Dressed in blue jeans, a tight white t-shirt, and a brown leather jacket, he looked nothing like the cop he had been that morning. At the sight of his casual attire, Caley felt herself relax. When Caley had dressed that morning in her ragged jeans and a new sweatshirt, she'd worried slightly that she would be underdressed. From the way that Owen was looking at her, she felt that she had made the right choice.

"Are you feeling better after your breakfast?" Owen asked, and he smiled when Caley nodded. "I thought we could wander around town and grab a bite at one of my favorite cafés. Then I have a surprise for you this afternoon if you're up for it," he added with a cheeky smile.

They strolled away from the bar and headed down the streets towards the town center. Owen drew her attention to his favorite haunts, places she'd missed noticing during her original walk. He showed her the bakery where they made the best apple Danish and the corner store where you could buy everything from fishing reels to cookbooks. Danishes in hand, they sat for a moment on a park bench donated in memory of the man who planted the first cherry trees. Two dogs, pulling their leads out of their owner's hands, came galloping in their direction and sniffed Caley all over. They licked her hands and pawed at her knees, demanding to be petted. She ruffled their ears and stroked their coats. She was pleased to see that Owen did not shy away from their attention and also happily patted the dogs. The owner came running over, apologizing profusely and both Caley and Owen brushed off the apology. Rather than feeling bad about the incident, Caley thought she should be thanking the woman. Now she knew for sure that Owen was a dog lover, another point in his favor.

Everywhere they went, Owen was greeted cheerfully and knew many of the townspeople by name. When they reached the small café called Get Stuffed, which specialized in mouthwatering spuds stuffed to overflowing with toppings, he enquired after the waitress's children and they chatted with ease. The only time anyone tried to avoid him was as they turned a corner into the main street and a teenager on a skateboard hurriedly changed direction at the sight of them. Caley watched Owen's lips tighten and saw his shoulder muscles tense, then relax. He muttered, quietly shaking his head, "He should be in school."

Throughout their walk and lunch date, Owen had been the perfect gentlemen. Each time Caley's arm brushed Owen's, she felt a tingle go through her, but she resisted the urge to take hold of his hand. She could still remember the feeling of her small hand in his large one. From the looks he gave her whenever their eyes met, she knew he was tempted. But he was holding himself back like she was. As if he was worried that if he came on too fast, he would startle her. That she would disappear again. She knew that if she wanted to take things further, it would be up to her to make the first move. But Caley just wasn't sure if she should. She knew what it was like to have her heartbroken, and wasn't sure if she could put him, or herself, through that. So she kept a space between them as they wandered and tried to ignore the invitation in his smile.

"Are you ready for your surprise?" Owen asked.

"I think so," Caley said, suddenly nervous.

"We could walk where we are going, but it is much quicker if we drive. Plus, I don't want you to be late for your first shift."

"Ok, but I don't have a car..." Caley's nerves were skyrocketing. If Owen's surprise involved driving, she was screwed. Despite what her fake ID said she didn't actually have her license. She'd left home at fifteen and being on the run didn't exactly give one much time to practice.

"No need. Mine is parked at the station. I can drive, but only if you feel confident about getting in a car with me?" Owen's smile, which had been broad and confident became hesitant.

"I'm fine. Really. I just don't like surprises," Caley reassured him.

"I could tell you but ... it might ruin it. We won't do anything that you don't feel comfortable with. Deal?" Owen held out his hand to her and she, hesitating only slightly, shook it. It was the type of handshake that went on for longer than required, but she found herself, once again, unwilling to withdraw her hand from his. He was like a magnet, unexpectedly drawing her to him.

The police station was located three streets back from the main strip. Owen's car turned out to be a dual-cab pickup truck in a neon blue. The open tray was empty except for two plastic trays, the kind they served food on at McDonald's, which Caley thought was a little odd. As they headed out of town towards the lake, she could hear them rattling as they slid from one side of the tray to the other. The noise was irritating, but Owen paid it no heed so she decided she could ignore it too. Reaching the coast road which separated the forested edge of the lake from the town, Owen turned right and up to a side road which inclined steeply, following the lines of the hills and dunes. On her way through the woods, Caley had come across a lookout, situated at the top which gave a magnificent view of Lake Michigan. She felt herself relax as she guessed their destination.

She was surprised, however, when reaching the top of the hill, Owen turned left onto a gravel road, instead of following the bitumen to the peak. After a few bumpy minutes, he parked the car off the side of the track, near two others. Getting out of the truck and gazing around, Caley could see nothing of interest in this particular location. The view was blocked by the top of the vast sand dunes. Turning, she saw that Owen was holding out the two plastic trays and that he had removed his jacket.

"Ready?" he asked, grinning broadly.

"For what?"

"Sandboarding," Owen said, holding one of the trays out to her. Then, before she had a chance to think, he grabbed her free hand and pulled her towards the dunes. Together they ran through the soft white sand, struggling a little as it tried to claim their feet until they reached the top of the closest dune. Looking down Caley gasped. A seemingly endless slope of white sand ran at a steep angle from the top of the dune to the shore of the lake.

"It's 300 feet from here to the shore. Makes for a fun slide if you are up for it. I will warn you though, after the thrill we will have to walk back up."

Caley's answer was to step forward, position her tray on the sand, and sit firmly in the center. Gripping the side of the tray, she looked up at Owen and, with a wink, said: "I'll race you to the bottom." She pushed herself off, and within seconds, she was flying down the dune. The fresh air blowing off the lake whipped her face, her red hair broke its restraints and streamed like a flame behind her. She screamed with delight, using her grip to curve the slide left and right, laughing as she careened over each bump. Her blood sang, and she fought the urge to reach inside for her magic, to heighten her human senses.

As the dune began to flatten, stretching out to touch the water, she turned to find Owen sliding to a stop beside her. His handsome face was flecked with sand, his hair windblown, and there were tears from the wind in his eyes. Also, like her, he was laughing. As her tray came to a halt, she reached for him and, wrapping her arms around his neck, kissed him fervently. His lips tasted of salt and were rough with sand, but she didn't care. She felt free. Free in a human way, and it was an experience to be savored.

Walking back up the dune, they stopped every dozen or so feet to kiss. Holding hands affected their balance, and often they fell in the soft sand, laughing. When they reached the top of the dune and saw the car, Caley couldn't help but feel a little disappointed. As if sensing her mood, Owen squeezed her hand.

"We can come back again. I promise."

"I'd really like that."

"Good," he kissed her again, this time slowly and tenderly, then pulled away. "But for now, we have to get you back in time for your shift." Looking her up and down, he added: "You need to change." Caley laughed. She would need a long shower to remove all the sand from her hair and skin.

"At least I won't have to worry about exfoliating for a while."

The journey back to the tavern was much shorter than Caley would have liked. They sat in comfortable silence, listening to the radio, holding hands. When they reached the parking lot, Owen opened her door for her and kissed her again. "Good luck with your first shift. I might see you tomorrow?" he asked, brushing a loose strand of hair from her forehead and tucking it behind her ear.

"I'd like that."

She waited outside the front door, waving as he drove away, feeling like she was floating. Pulling open the heavy door, she headed towards the stairs but suddenly stopped short. A television above the bar displayed a news broadcast. It showed a picture of a missing girl with urgent calls for anyone with information to contact the police. She had chestnut hair, a long nose and brown eyes framed with chestnut lashes. "Hannah," Caley murmured, moments before her full name flashed across the screen. The hair on the back of Caley's neck rose, and a growl escaped unbidden from her throat. She had never met the girl, but she felt like she had, many a night in her dreams.

CHAPTER 4

Caley's first shift went by in a daze. She was sure that Melody had instantly regretted hiring her. All that prevented Caley from making a complete fool of herself that first night was the months of waitressing experience she had under her belt. It hadn't, however, saved her from the hideous embarrassment of pouring a beer into a customer's lap. She'd been sliding the foam-topped lager across the bar when a news update flashed across the television screen capturing her attention. Hannah's family's appeal would replay on the 11 o'clock news. The $50,000 reward, offered in return for any information that would help find her, blared across the screen. Accompanying the update was another photo of Hannah, her arms wrapped around the neck of a large black horse, smiling and radiating joy. Her wide eyes seemed to be staring directly into Caley's soul.

After grabbing a cloth to stem the flow, and apologizing profusely to the man, Caley tried to keep her focus on her work and ignore the television. As more patrons flooded into the pub, she found it became easier to focus on the job, the sound of their chatter blocking out the noise from the television. When the news report came on, she was too busy clearing tables to pay much attention. But as the clock struck midnight and Melody locked the door, ushering the last of the customers out, Caley found her thoughts once again returning to the missing girl. Mistaking her distraction for tiredness, Melody told her to head upstairs and go to bed.

"I'm sorry about the spill," Caley apologized yet again, undoing the half apron from around her waist and hanging it back on the hook. Pulling the bottle opener and dishcloth from the pockets, she threw them on the tray for cleaning.

"Don't worry about it, love. No one ever has a great first shift, and you're still finding your feet. A good night's sleep will do you a world of good," Melody said as she grabbed a damp cloth and started to wipe the beer stains off the bar.

Gratefully Caley headed up the stairs. Grabbing her towel from her room, she headed for the communal bathroom, desperate for a shower. As the hot water soaked her skin, she tried to let it wash her edginess away. But while it felt heavenly on her sore muscles, it did nothing for her mind. Caley couldn't shake the feeling that she knew Hannah; even though there was no possible way that she could ever have met her. The news report had said the girl was from Texas, a place Caley had never been. Maybe Hannah just had one of those familiar faces that always looked like someone else? Perhaps Caley had met someone who looked like her? Drying herself and wrapping her towel around her, she headed back to her room trying to think of who she had met with the face that was so much like Hannah's.

Turning off the light and slipping into bed, Caley tried once again to empty her mind. She closed her eyes and counted backward from 100, an old habit that often worked to help her drift off to sleep. But tonight Caley reached zero and still the escape of sleep evaded her. Sighing she rolled onto her side and tried counting sheep. Instead of helping it only made her laugh. Partly because it was such a cliché, and partly because she could turn into a wolf, so dreaming of sheep was more likely to make her restless than give her the deep, dreamless sleep she craved. Rolling over onto her back, she tried to find a comfortable position. The bed was soft, and yet nothing felt right. She considered changing form. A dog would fit comfortably on the bed without the risk of breaking it as her wolf form would. A fox would be even lighter. Getting out of bed, she double-checked to ensure she had locked her bedroom door. She had. Climbing back under the sheet, she decided that if she hadn't fallen asleep within half an hour, she would change.

Whether it was the self-imposed time limit or her body giving in to the exhaustion, sleep took hold of Caley before she changed form. But her dreams were restless. Caley tossed and turned repeatedly. She dreamed she was being chased through a dark field by a man dressed in black. Caley couldn't make out his face but knew that if he caught her, he would kill her. The landscape she ran through was barren, no trees or cover to hide behind. As fast as Caley sprinted, the man kept gaining on her. She attempted to change form but couldn't. She tried to scream, but no words came out.

Then Owen suddenly appeared. Dressed in the same outfit he had worn that day, he was smiling at her, unaware of the danger. She tried to call out to him, to scream for him to run, but nothing happened. She tried signaling him, but it was like he couldn't see her. A loud crack ripped through the dream and in front of her Owen's chest exploded as a barrel full of bullets tore through it. Blood spurted out from the wound, covering her in a spray of red. His body slumped to the ground. Reaching him, she stumbled, falling so that she landed next to him. Her face was inches from his, his eyes wide and staring with the blankness of the dead. She opened her mouth and screamed silently into the night.

With a jerk of pain, she felt the hunter grab her shoulder, pulling her up and flipping her over. She still couldn't make out his face as he knelt on her chest, holding her down. She struggled to throw him off, but he was too strong. Leaning over her, so close she could feel his warm breath on her face, she felt the icy touch of a blade as he held it against her throat. As it started to slice through the tender flesh of her neck, she woke, sitting bolt upright in bed, screaming at the top of her lungs. Sweat dripped down her body, making the sheet cling to her naked skin in damp clumps. While she was asleep, her hands must have become claws for there were tears in the bottom layer and part of the top sheet was in tatters. The blanket was saved only because during her tossing and turning; she had somehow thrown it to the floor.

Gasping for air, she pressed one hand to her throat,

half expecting to find it a ruined mess. Instead, she found it whole, but clammy. The knife had felt so real. Feeling light-headed, Caley realized she was hyperventilating and tried to calm her breathing. One by one, she took in her surroundings, using reality to push away the lingering fragments of the dream. She became aware that it must be nearing a full moon as its light made a path from the window across the wooden floor. Perhaps it was the cause of the dream. Her wolf self reacting to its call. Looking at the floor, she made out her shoes where she had left them by the door, her towel, which was draped over the foot of her bed, her purse hanging from the door handle. A flicker of light caught the corner of her eye, making her turn towards the empty bed across the room. Only it wasn't empty anymore.

Sitting on the bed, legs crossed in front of her, sat a woman dressed in a pale blue tunic and shorts. Her thick, dark hair fell in a braid down one shoulder, and she played with it, twisting the ends in her fingers. Her skin was more golden than tan, her eyes which watched Caley were the deep blue of an ocean at night. A band of fine gold encircled her brow, a matching cuff on each wrist. In her lap lay a wooden bow, on the bed next to her a quiver of feather fletched arrows. But it wasn't all this that made Caley scream. It was the fact that the woman was glowing and, scarier still, even in the dark, Caley could make out the texture of the brick wall behind her. Through her.

"Will you please stop screaming, you're starting to give me a headache," the woman said in a waspish yet melodic voice, "Caley there are things we need to talk about, and it won't happen if you're making such an idiotic noise."

CHAPTER 5

"Who the hell are you?" Caley demanded. "What the hell are you?" Caley tore her gaze away from the glowing woman sitting on the bed to scan the door. It was definitely still locked from the inside. "How did you get in my room?"

"So many questions and yet you are not asking the right questions. Also," the woman gestured to herself, encompassing the bow which lay across her lap, "I'm sure you already know who I am."

"An intruder dressed up as a cosplayer?" Caley guessed. It was the only semi-logical thing her startled brain could come up with. The other thought was a ghost, and that was just plain ridiculous.

"Seriously, what are they teaching you in schools these days?" The woman said with a sigh, shaking her head. Sitting up straighter, pushing her shoulders back and tilting up her head, she announced, "I am Artemis. Goddess of the Moon and the Hunt."

Caley couldn't help it, she burst out laughing and, after

the terror of her dream, it felt so good to laugh she couldn't stop. If looks could kill the one the golden woman gave would have turned Caley to ash in an instant, but since it couldn't kill it only worked to make Caley laugh harder. Here she was, naked in bed apart from a torn sheet wrapped haphazardly around her sitting across from a woman who claimed to be an ancient Greek goddess. Realizing she must still be dreaming, she waited to wake up. At least this dream was funnier than the last one.

"I'm sorry," Caley said, trying to get her laughter under control, "It's a pleasure to meet you ... Artemis." Another giggle escaped as she said the name.

"This is not going as I expected," the goddess said, looking peeved.

"What did you expect? That you would appear and I would bow down to you?" Caley asked, smiling broadly.

"Yes, as you should. My brother Apollo is right, humankind has become full of heathens now." Artemis shook her head. "At the very least, you could thank me."

"Thank you for what?" Caley asked. This dream was getting stranger and stranger.

"For your gifts. For your connection to the Canidae. The wolves, dogs, you know, your ability to become one of them." Artemis said.

"Gift? Is that what you call it? If you are the one who gave it to me that last thing I would ever want to do is thank you. This ability has cost me my family and everyone I care about," Caley responded, all traces of humor gone.

"Yes. Well, that wasn't supposed to happen. I blame

technology and social media." Her full lips pursed as if she had tasted something sour. "Other generations have worshipped me for their gifts. In 1866, the last time the moons aligned, one of my descendants embraced her gifts, and her great deeds inspired the first national parks. Everyone thinks it was her teammate William Jackson who took the photographs. But the real question is who inspired him to take them? One of you. One of my huntresses."

Caley was baffled. This dream was making no sense at all. Reaching down, she pinched the skin on the back of her right hand hard enough for it to sting, but it didn't wake her up. Not seeming to notice the golden woman continued, "Actually that is why I am here. I have a quest for you."

"A quest?" Caley asked. Was this woman serious?

"Yes. I need you to go and find your sisters and warn them that they are in danger. That they are being hunted."

"I think you have me confused with someone else," Caley said, part of her mind wondering why she was trying to contradict a dream. "I don't have sisters, plural. I have one sister, Emily, and she's safe at home with my parents."

"I'm not talking about your human family," Artemis replied, as though her reference should have been obvious. "I'm talking about your sister huntresses. The ones who are going missing. This horrible business must be stopped, and the only way for that to happen is for you to all work together. Combine your gifts."

"Well, why don't you contact them yourself and warn them?" Caley asked.

"Because I can't. I shouldn't be here now. If the other gods find out that I contacted you, there will be an uproar. We're not supposed to interfere in human lives."

"Then, why me?"

"Because I've watched you all your life," Artemis said.

"Wow, that doesn't sound creepy at all," Caley said, feeling the skin on the back of her neck prickle.

"I care about you. I care about all my huntresses. But you are the smartest of them all Caley. You are the one who sensed the danger and ran. I watched you protect yourself. Hide. I know you can teach your sisters to do the same."

"Maybe I'm tired of running," Caley admitted. She thought of Owen, his smile, his kind eyes, the way it had felt when he had kissed her.

"No, no, no," Artemis admonished waving a perfectly manicured finger at her. "Do not let yourself get distracted by a man. Men only mean trouble. He'll only slow you down. Break your heart. Get you killed. Distract you."

"Distract me from what?"

"Your quest," Artemis sighed in exasperation. "Are you not listening to me at all?"

"I'm sorry, but whatever it is you want I'm not the right person for it. I'm not really a team player. Making friends just leads to having to let them go. You are going to have to find someone else to complete your damned quest."

"There is no one else. If you don't do this, then your sisters will die. All of them, not just the dozen they have

MIRANDA HARVEY & & CATE ALEXANDER

already captured and slain. They have Hannah. Don't you care?"

"Hannah?" Caley asked, the photograph of the missing girl with her horse becoming clear in her mind.

"Yes, Hannah. She has the gift of the Equine. You have to find her."

"Ahhhh." Finally, it was all making sense. Somehow her mind had taken the news about the missing girl and combined it with own terror of being hunted and conjured this strange dream. Even the nonsensical could make sense when you could put it all into context.

Taking this as acceptance, Artemis smiled broadly at Caley.

"See, I knew you'd understand. I knew I could rely on you to find the others," Reaching into the quiver Artemis pulled out one of the arrows. With a twist and a pull, she removed the arrow's tip which gleamed like silver in the moonlight. Reaching over, she handed it to Caley. Caley was surprised how cold and solid it felt in the palm of her hand. So real. "Take this arrowhead. When you hold it in your palm, it will lead you to your sisters. I'm trusting you with this Caley. Please don't let me down."

"I won't," Caley said. It felt strange to promise something to a figment of her own imagination. But dream promises didn't count so that was okay and perhaps that is what it would take to wake her from this strange dream. Caley really wanted to wake up. Or to fall into a night of deep, dreamless sleep.

"Good," Artemis smiled broadly again. "I knew I made the right choice in picking you, and I'm always right. I better go before Apollo realizes I'm missing and has a hissy fit. Also, you need your sleep. You have a big job ahead of you, and you'll need all your energy. Go with my blessing. Your sisters depend on you." Standing up from the bed, the goddess stepped closer to Caley, leaning forward to plant a gentle kiss on the center of her brow. The touch of her lips felt cool against Caley's clammy forehead, and the scent of roses and honeysuckle wafted from the goddess' hair. But Caley had only a millisecond to wonder at this detail before sleep, like a wave, overtook her.

Her restless night had thrown out her usually reliable internal alarm clock. When she did wake, checking her watch, she was startled to see that she had only twenty minutes before her shift was due to start. In a rush she pulled on her clothes, scraping her red hair into an untidy bun atop her head as she did so. Picking up her toiletries bag, she was about to run to the bathroom when the sight of her bed made her pause. If anyone happened to see the torn bedsheets, it would lead to questions she couldn't answer. Grabbing up the blanket, she laid it over the sheets, spreading it to hide the evidence. Adjusting her pillow, she failed to notice the silver arrowhead which lay tucked beneath it, placed there by the goddess after it had dropped from Caley's limp hand as she had fallen into sleep.

CHAPTER 6

C aley wished she had time for a shower, but upon checking her watch, she saw there were only ten minutes before she needed to be downstairs in the bar. Running the tap and filling her cupped hands with cold water, she splashed her face. Caley could feel the icy water beginning to chase away some of the grogginess. Squeezing a line of paste onto her toothbrush, she started to brush her teeth vigorously. Her mouth felt like cardboard, but even if it hadn't her daily dental routine was never something she missed. Fake social security, combined with being on the run, did not lend itself to convenient dental care.

Looking in the mirror, she was a little surprised not to see an imprint of lips in the middle of her forehead. She barely remembered the nightmare, but the one about the goddess, Artemis she'd called herself, was startlingly clear. It was like Caley could still feel the point on her brow where the goddess had kissed her. So strange. Plus, what had the goddess meant about Caley being a huntress? More like hunted. Dreams were so weird.

Her morning shift went more smoothly than that of the previous night. She didn't spill a single drink, on a customer or otherwise, and remembered all the breakfast and lunch orders without having to write them down. She even impressed one of the regulars by making him a Tickled Peach, a trick she'd picked up when she was in Wyoming. It was just a hint of bourbon and peach schnapps mixed with cola, but damn it was good. By the time her lunch break came, she was feeling pretty relaxed, the terror and strangeness of the previous night wholly forgotten. Caley sat in one of the booths, enjoying her lunch and reading a gossip magazine a customer had left behind when she heard a familiar voice call her name. Looking up, she found Owen, dressed in his uniform, smiling down at her. She was relieved not to feel the fear that had previously rushed over her when she'd realized he was a cop; instead, she just felt happiness at seeing him.

"Hi," she said, gesturing to the seat opposite her in invitation. "Want to join me?"

"I can't. I have to be back at the station in ten. But I wanted to ask if you have any plans for tonight?"

"Not one. Hard to have plans when you don't know anyone."

"Would you like to have dinner with me?" Owen asked, his broad smile suddenly turning shy. Caley's mind flew to her quickly dwindling funds. She wanted to spend time with Owen but didn't want to go out knowing she wouldn't be able to pay for her share of the night. As if sensing her concern, Owen smiled shyly. "The owner of the Apple & Grape Winery owes me a favor. He's been pushing me to come by and claim the free dinner he promised me but, well, I've never really had anyone to go with."

Caley knew she should say no. She would be leaving soon, and she didn't want to lead him on, to break his heart. But there was something so beguiling about the way he smiled as he asked her, the way a dimple appeared in his left cheek and how Owen played with his hands as if nervous, that she couldn't resist. He was precisely the kind of man her parents would approve of. Thinking about how she'd never get the chance to introduce him to them made her sad. But she could at least do this. She could go on a date with a man that she could present to her parents in a different reality. Screw it. She could have dinner with him. Just once.

"I'd love to," she said.

The grin he gave her was like sunshine. "I'll pick you up about 6.30? I thought we could catch a cab since wine tasting will also be included."

"That sounds wonderful."

"Alright, I'll see you then." Owen seemed to hesitate for a moment, and she thought he was about to ask her something else, so she was surprised when instead he leaned down and kissed her softly on the cheek. "See you tonight," he said, blushing slightly.

That night Caley took extra care getting ready. As soon as she had finished her shift, she had rushed to splurge some of her last remaining dollars on a simple but cute mid-sleeved dress. It was green, which brought out the color of her eyes, and the golden and orange leaves sprinkled over the bodice went well with her hair. She never wore much makeup, never really had the need, but she used mascara and lip gloss and brushed her hair so that it hung like a burning flame. She'd asked Melody about the venue, and she hoped her outfit would be suitable for the vineyard and restaurant. She didn't want to look a fool or disappoint Owen. Melody assured her she looked perfect and lent her a vintage purse and some simple gold jewelry. Caley felt much more confident with those finishing touches and wondered again just how much Mel could sense about her. Picking up her cardigan, her jacket far too shabby to wear with her dress, she wrapped it around her shoulders. The night was already starting to get chilly, but Caley hoped the cardigan would be enough to suffice if they stayed inside. Thoughts of the freezing winter to come threatened to overtake her happy mood, but she thrust them aside. Just for tonight, Caley was going to enjoy herself. She was going to remember what it meant to be a normal human woman.

The nod and smile of approval Melody gave her as she came downstairs for a final twirl helped boost her confidence. She was glad she had decided to buy the dress. Glad she'd ignored her overwhelming need for privacy and let Melody help her with the finishing touches. She sat at the bar while David, the bartender whose job she was taking, poured her a glass of wine. He passed it to her. "Owen is a lucky man. If things don't work out, I'm still here for another couple of weeks." His words made her blush, but the over-exaggerated wink that followed made her laugh. Whether things worked out or not, she would be gone in less than two weeks. Caley was taking the last sip of her wine when the bell above the door rang. Spinning on her bar stool, she saw it was Owen pushing open the heavy door. He was dressed in cream pants, a navy collared shirt, open at the throat, no tie, and a warm grey wool jacket. His hair had been brushed back, and as he came closer, she could smell the cologne he wore, a mix of sandalwood, cedar, and a touch of something citrus.

"You look beautiful," Owen said, his shining brown eyes roaming appreciatively over her, but not lingering on any one spot too long.

"So do you," she said and then lowered her eyes as heat rush to her head, her embarrassment making her feel flushed. She was really out of practice. Owen probably thought her a simpleton.

"Thanks," Owen smiled, before reaching out a hand to her. The cab waited outside the pub for them, and they climbed into the back, Owen opening the door for Caley. They sat in silence for most of the twenty-minute journey, both suddenly shy, but still holding hands. Looking at the sky, Caley thought it was going to be a beautiful sunset, the sun making its slow way down towards the horizon, turning the clouds blush-pink.

The stone sign at the head of the gate displayed a picture of an apple and a grape dancing, making Caley smile. The long gravel drive leading into the vineyard was bordered by apple trees, their branches and trunks strung with tiny lights, so they looked to be adorned with dancing fireflies. As they approached the parking lot, she could hear music. Once the cab pulled to a stop, Owen paid the driver and then got out of the car, coming around to open Caley's door for her. Yes, her parents definitely would have approved. Taking her hand once again he led her down a stone path, this time bordered with dark ornamental plum trees once again strung with lights. They came to a crossroads. The wooden sign indicated that the cellar door was to their left and the restaurant to their right. Owen looked at his watch.

"We have time if you want to do a wine or a mulled cider tasting before dinner?" he offered.

"Sure," she said. Perhaps the alcohol would work to calm the butterflies which were dancing up a storm in her belly. It might also work to drown out the inner voice which kept telling her that there was something else, something important, that she was supposed to be doing.

They turned left and before long came to a building which reminded Caley of cabins she'd seen deep in the woods, only far more luxurious. The walls were made out of river stones, each one unique and polished so it gleamed. The roof, porch, and banisters were carved out of oak. While the porch's floorboards were smooth, the rest had been left in their natural form, adding to the building's rustic air. Empty wine barrels and chairs scattered the porch, inviting patrons to sit for a while and have a drink. The theme continued inside with polished concrete floors, a large polished oak bar, and more wine barrels and chairs. A fireplace crackled taking the chill from the air and warming the handful of guests seated around it. Behind the bar, stretching from one wall to the other, were hundreds of wine bottles, too many for Caley to count. In front stood four double-doored fridges filled to the brim with bottles. Behind the bar stood a woman, in her mid-thirties, slightly plump with a short dark bob, a snub nose, and a warm smile.

"Hello, Owen. Finally taking Victor up on his offer, I see," she said in a friendly voice.

"Just so he can stop nagging me," Owen responded with a laugh. "Danielle, this is Caley. She's new in town." Danielle held out a hand, and Caley shook it.

"What would you two like to start with? Mulled cider or wine?" Turning to Caley, she added, "We make both here from our own grapes and apples." Caley didn't think it would be a good idea to mix the two together in her already anxious stomach.

"Just wine for me, please. Red?"

"Easy done, Owen?"

"I'll stick to wine too. Although, Caley," he added with a smile in her direction, "We'll have to make another trip here someday. They make the most amazing hard ginger and lemongrass cider. Better we save it for summer though." As Danielle went to fetch the bottles of red, Caley thought wistfully of summer. It would be so lovely to spend so long in one place. Not just for the cider but for Owen's company which she had to admit she was enjoying more with every moment. But it couldn't happen. Even if she stayed until after winter, as soon as the snow cleared, she would have to leave.

Staying too long in one place would only lead to trouble. Like it in Montana. Thinking of Montana still gave her the chills. She thought she'd been safe in the town of Helena and had loved the thrill of racing across the mountain in wolf form. She'd gotten a job at Bad Betty's Barbecue for the winter, and when spring had come, they'd begged her to stay. She hadn't seen the harm in it. She'd made friends, the owners treated her like family, and the customers were always kind. She'd even been thinking about taking a night course to learn book-keeping and had filled in her details online for the course application. That had been her mistake.

Coming home after a late shift, she almost didn't notice the scratches on the door until it was too late. Her key had already been in the lock, and she had started turning the handle when some deeper instinct kicked in. Perhaps she'd heard a noise from inside her apartment. So, without opening the door, she had turned and fled, telling herself that it was her overactive imagination. That she was being ridiculous. That she must have left a window open. But when she saw the black Jeep in the parking lot, the one with the Arizona plates, she'd known she was right. She'd made it halfway across the lot when she heard a man's voice call out.

Turning around, she saw him, standing on the balcony outside of her apartment. Dressed all in black. Black pants, black shirt, black protective vest. He had raised a gun and pointed it at her, yelling for her to stop. But she ignored him, turning to flee. Some part of her knew that he wouldn't shoot, that whoever they were they wanted her alive. The hunter had sprinted down the stairs, he was fast, so fast, but not as fast as she was. Not in her wolf form. Just like that, she had shifted and run, disappearing into the national park, going off the grid. At the thought of how close she had come to being caught, she felt a shiver travel down her spine.

"Caley?" Owen asked, snapping her out of her memories. "Are you alright?"

"What? Yes. I'm fine. Sorry," Caley said, trying to shake off the fear that the memory had brought on.

"Poor girl looks dead on her feet," Danielle said in a sympathetic voice.

"I didn't sleep very well last night," Caley admitted.

"And then you worked today. You should have told me, we could have headed straight to dinner so you could sit down and relax," Owen said, his brow creased with concern.

"I'm alright, truly. I think I just need a drink."

"That I can help you with," Danielle said, smiling and holding up two bottles. "Do you want to start with the Pinot Noir or the Tempranillo?"

"Tempranillo, please."

Danielle poured them both a generous taste into the waiting wine glasses. Picking up his, Owen waited until Caley had her glass before saying, "A toast. To the first of many pleasant nights." In response, Caley forced a smile as she clinked her glass against his before taking a sip. The wine tasted like cherries, but it did little to warm the chill that had settled over Caley.

CHAPTER 7

fter tasting four of the vineyard's superb wines, Caley had to admit that she was feeling better. Danielle had told them about the history of the winery and the inspiration for each vintage. She made it sound like magic. Holding Owen's hand as they walked to the restaurant afterward, she could almost imagine she had stepped into a fantasy world.

But she soon discovered that if she had thought that the tasting room was luxurious, it was nothing compared to the restaurant. The wood and stone theme had been continued, but the rustic wine barrels had been replaced with leather chairs and solid walnut tables. Wildflowers and lit candles decorated the tables, and the whole place sparkled with more of the tiny, almost magical lights. But its most impressive feature was the view. Whoever had designed the building had positioned it so that every diner, no matter where they sat, had an entrancing view of the vineyard and orchard.

Victor, the owner, had greeted them at the entrance,

giving Caley a kiss on each cheek and Owen a hug. He led them to a table right near the enormous glass window so they would have an unobstructed view. While they had been enjoying the wine-tasting, the sun had begun to set. As Owen pulled out her chair and she took her seat, Caley's gaze was captured by the final, glowing rays of sunlight across the scenery below.

"I hope you don't mind, but I've asked the chef to prepare our specialties for you. Plus, there is a matched glass of wine to go with each course," Victor said, looking a little nervous. When they both nodded their approval, he smiled widely, flashing two gold teeth. "Good, good. But first, you don't have any allergies, do you?"

"No," Caley answered while Owen just shook his head.

"Wonderful. I will let the chef know we can proceed as planned. If you need anything, anything at all, just let me know," he said before giving them a slight bow and disappearing.

"Exactly what did you do to earn Victor's favor?" Caley asked, looking around. Their table had not been set with menus but looking at the meals being enjoyed around them, she knew it wouldn't be cheap.

"It's kind of a long story," Owen warned.

"Victor mentioned courses. I think we have plenty of time," Caley returned not giving up. She wanted, craved, to know more about Owen. To know the sort of man he really was.

"Well a place like this, it takes a lot of hands, especially at harvest time. There aren't enough locals looking for work, so Victor tends to hire backpackers, travelers from out of state. He pays them well with cash to keep it simple, and usually, he doesn't have a problem."

Owen paused as a waiter appeared with their first course. A stone jar filled with chicken liver pâté, accompanied by a Riesling apple cinnamon jelly and freshly baked black bread which was crunchy on the outside and soft in the center. A waitress followed behind him carrying two half glasses of a berry Riesling. As they spread bits of bread with the parfait, Owen continued, "But unfortunately, that wasn't the case with the most recent apple picking."

Between mouthfuls of the delicious food and pauses to enjoy the view, Owen continued the story. "The team had been out in the orchards when one of the tour buses stopped by. Usually, they are full of middle-aged tourists, but this one was packed with very drunk men on a bachelor party. They had two," Owen paused for a second, brow furrowed, "scantily-clad ladies with them. When they tried to get into the tasting room, Danielle denied them entry, and they weren't too happy about it."

"So you were called in to convince them?" Caley guessed, sighing with pleasure as she finished the last sip of the delicious wine.

"If only it had been that easy. No. I'm afraid things escalated out of control." Owen paused once again as a waiter came to clear their dishes, followed on his heels by another waiter carrying a plate of fried goats' cheese in apple blossom honey and two half-glasses of Chardonnay. Breaking into one of the balls of cheese with a fork Caley dipped it in the syrup before popping it into her mouth. The saltiness of the cheese balanced perfectly with the sweet honey while the wine cleared her palette ready for the next bite.

"Mmmmm, this is wonderful," she murmured to Owen between mouthfuls. "So, what happened next?"

"Danielle is used to handling drunks, and the incident probably would have ended there had the picking team not happened to pass the car park as the men were returning to their bus. Women make great pickers with their smaller hands, and the men took a liking to one of the girls, Monique, a sweet thing, barely twenty-one. She was Spanish, and her English is pretty heavily accented, but I'd hazard a guess she was making her refusal pretty clear. Either way, they weren't taking no for an answer." Owen shook his head, wincing at the unpleasant memory.

"They tried to drag her away, clamping a hand over her mouth when she tried to scream so Sven, one of the men in the picking team, decided to intervene. The fight alerted vineyard security but not in time to stop Sven from breaking the best man's nose. The place was in an uproar, guests all putting in their two cents worth and the drunks threatening to sue. The best man wanted to press charges, but Sven was working illegally, no work visa, and Victor was freaking out. Danielle called me."

Caley jumped as a hand suddenly appeared in front of her, picking up the empty plate. She'd been so engrossed in Owen's story she'd utterly lost awareness of their surroundings. Even though the waiter behind him held a plate beautifully decorated with salmon gravlax, fennel, juniper, radish, and beets, she wanted for nothing more than for them to hurry up and move away. She barely tasted the pink rosé which was placed before her, as she asked, "So what did you do?"

"I convinced the guy with the broken nose that it would be in his best interest not to press charges for assault. Getting arrested for alleged rape doesn't look so good on your job applications. And I pointed out that while Sven had a group of sober, responsible witnesses, his supporters were all drunk and could be charged with being complicit. I also said that I would book Sven for the night as a result of his actions. While Victor offered everyone in the restaurant a free round of drinks, I escorted Sven to the car, and we drove around the block a few times while we waited for the tour bus to leave. As soon as they did, I drove Sven back here, and he snuck around the back to the pickers' quarters, no one the wiser. The next day Victor called to thank me and offered me a free meal on the house. I tried to refuse, but he insisted and, well, here we are."

Caley took a sip of her wine, actually tasting it this time, and marveled at the way Owen brushed off his heroism. In her experience, cops weren't good at taking the harder road and defending the innocent. Most would have said yes to the drunks from the tour bus, who were wealthy and privileged, rather than protecting the pickers. Most would have arrested Sven for not only assaulting the best man but for working illegally. Instead, Owen chose to protect Sven, dropping him back without charging him.

As the next course arrived, pork tenderloin with saffron and apple purée paired with a glass of the delicious Tempranillo she had tasted before, Owen redirected the conversation to Caley, "Enough about me. Tell me about you. Tell me about your family."

Usually, Caley was guarded about her personal life, mentioning only the sparest of details generally with a twist of deceit mixed in with the truth. She wasn't sure if it was the wine, or that some part of her didn't want to lie to Owen, but she found herself telling him about her real family.

"My mum is a school teacher and the best cook. Not as good as Victor's chef, but her lasagna is drool-worthy. My dad is a mechanic, he's never met an engine he couldn't fix. I have two siblings, both younger than me. Matthew is into sports, mainly football and plays quarterback for his school's team, while Emily is the complete opposite. She's artistic and plays the piano."

"And you? What are you into?" Owen inquired. Such a simple question and yet it made Caley pause. What was she into? Staying alive, turning into a wolf, existing.

"I like to run, and I like animals," she answered awkwardly.

"What about dancing?" Owen asked.

"Dancing?" The question startled her. "I've never really learned." She'd never finished high school, never had a chance to go to prom. She'd bopped around to music in a bar, but she didn't think that was what he meant.

Owen stood up from the table, folding his napkin and placing it next to his plate. Holding out a hand, he asked, "Then how about we try?"

Owen led her to the center of the restaurant where a small dance floor was set up. Two older couples, both in their seventies, swirled around the floor. Classical music

Caley couldn't name floated down from speakers hidden in the ceiling. Leading her to the middle of the dance floor, Owen placed one hand on her waist, keeping hold of her other hand. Slowly they began to sway to the music. Caley looked at her feet, paranoid about stepping on Owen's toes.

"Don't look at your feet. Just trust me. I won't lead you wrong," Owen said, his voice soft. Looking up, she saw him smiling at her, and her lips formed a smile in return. Lifting his hand, he guided her into a spin, the skirts of her dress twirling around her, making her laugh. One of the gentleman dancers caught her eye and smiled at her. Pulling her back to him, closer this time, Owen whispered into her ear, his breath warm against her cheek, "See you can dance just fine." One song ended, and another began; they continued to dance. Other younger couples, closer to their own age, joined them on the floor and by the time the third song started more than a dozen couples danced. Yet Caley hardly noticed them, caught up in the feel of Owen's hand on her waist, his warm brown eyes making her whole body tingle. She'd not noticed before how they were flecked with gold, how simple it was to get lost in them when he looked at her like that. Like he could see all the way to her soul.

Caley couldn't be sure how long they danced, but it must have been at least 10 or 12 songs before they headed back to their table. A plate covered in tiny cakes and pastries waited for them as well as a bottle of dessert wine. Reaching instead for her glass of water Caley took a couple of large swallows.

"How about we see if we can get this to go and go for a

walk? There's a path through the vines that is beautiful at this time of year. Up here there are so few lights that you can really see how stunning the sky is at night. Absolutely full of stars."

"I'd love that," Caley answered without hesitation. She didn't want the night to end, wasn't ready to go back to the pub and risk another night of unsettling dreams. She would much rather stay here with Owen in what felt like the sweetest dream she'd ever had.

Owen called a waiter who readily agreed, a slight smirk on his face. While they waited for him to wrap it all up, Victor came over. "Everything was acceptable?" he asked nervously.

"It was delicious," Owen reassured him.

"It was perfect," Caley added, unsure if she was refer-ring the beautiful food, the delicious wine or Owen's company.

"Good. I hope to see you both again soon. No reserva-tion required, just let my staff know, and we will always find you a table." With a slight bow and a broad smile, he left them, wandering through the other tables, greeting most of the guests by name.

Once the waiter returned with their food, the bottle of wine and two plastic cups, they made their exit. Instead of going down the path they had taken to reach the main entrance, Owen guided Caley to a path which wound behind the restaurant. Caley noticed a large river stone with the words "Vineyard walk. Please follow the stones," painted in luminous ink which caught the moonlight. Looking ahead, Caley spotted the next stone outlining the path for them to follow.

Owen confidently guided them along the path, and for a moment, she wondered how many other girls he had taken on this same walk. Perhaps he did this all the time. Yet, somehow, she didn't think so. There was something too sweet about him for her to believe him a player. His friend Mike maybe, but not Owen. It made her a little sad, hoping that once she left, this perfect night wouldn't ruin his chance to share this with someone else. Someone who deserved this type of happiness with Owen. The thought of him with someone else sent a stab of pain shooting into her heart. But she knew she would have to leave, one day, and it was selfish to claim Owen as hers when he could never be hers, no matter how much she wanted him to be.

CHAPTER 8

There were other couples taking advantage of the privacy of the vineyard, but they managed to find a quiet spot to sit down. The ground was covered in soft grass, and despite the chill, Caley found she didn't care in the slightest if she got grass stains on her new dress. Lying down, the open container of desserts between them, they stared up the stars. Caley had never studied astronomy, another thing she'd missed out on moving from place to place, so Owen pointed out the constellations to her, telling her the story behind each one. There were the two bears of Ursa, the twins of Gemini and the swimming fish of Pisces. Her favorite was Canis Major, the dog. Caley had to resist the urge to bark, giggling as she thought about it.

"What star sign are you?" Owen asked.

"Sagittarius," she said and shivered as she remembered the golden woman from her dream with the bow and arrow.

"Well we can't see that constellation from here but see

there," he pointed to three stars which aligned in a row, "That is Orion's belt. His constellation can be seen from anywhere in the world. It is said that he was a supernatural hunter, the son of Poseidon and that he hunted with the Goddess of the Hunt, Artemis."

"Artemis?" Caley asked, startled at the mention of her dream woman's name. She had thought her a figment of her own imagination.

"She was the twin sister of the god Apollo. He ruled the sun while she ruled the moon," Owen laughed, misinterpreting Caley's wide-eyed look. "Now you think me some kind of history geek, don't you? But I can't help it. My mom is a history professor at the University of Wisconsin. Go Badgers," he finished with a fist pump in the air.

Caley's head was spinning, and this time she knew it wasn't because of the wine. Hadn't the woman in her dream mentioned an Apollo? Yet she was pretty sure that until last night she hadn't heard either name before. It wasn't like they tended to pop up in the paper. And if the names were real, did that mean that the rest of the dream was also real? She tried to remember the exact words of their conversation but found she couldn't. Something about a gift and a quest. She felt her heart start to beat faster, her fight or flight reaction trying to kick in. The urge to run. Yet she fought it. She would not let some fear ruin this perfect night. So, to distract herself, she rolled to face Owen and, placing a hand behind his head, pulled him closer and claimed his mouth with hers, not only wanting him but also wanting the distraction his kiss provided.

Their kisses on the sand dunes had been gentle, tentative, and sweet. This kiss was none of those things. It was passionate, hungry, and hard. It was intended to clear Caley's mind of all thought of anything except Owen, and it succeeded. Holding onto her waist, Owen rolled onto his back, pulling Caley with him. Her entire body lay against him, touched him, fitted to his. The cold night air against her back contrasted with the warmth of his body pressing against her, making her shiver in delight. Owen's hands roamed her lower back, her shoulders, her arms. He cupped her buttocks gently in his hands but didn't let them travel any further; despite the fact she probably would have allowed him.

"You are beautiful and amazing, and as much as I don't want to stop, we should. Before someone sees us," Owen said, breaking the kiss, his voice husky, "I don't want to, but, even off duty, I'm still a cop." He shrugged awkwardly.

Caley flushed; all thoughts of Artemis gone. Her blood was thrumming. She didn't want to stop. She craved to drown in the moment, never come up for air. Yet some part of her brain acknowledged the logic in Owen's words. "Alright," she said.

Standing up they both took a moment to brush off the bits of grass which clung to their clothes. Owen reached and pulled a leaf out of the strands of her hair, leaning forward to plant a kiss on her cheek as he did so. Picking up the now empty dessert container and the unopened bottle of wine, they headed back towards the entrance. Pulling his phone out of his pocket, Owen dialed the number of the cab company.

"They'll be about ten minutes," he informed her. They sat together waiting, holding hands on the stone wall which edged the car park.

"Tell me about your family?" Caley asked, trying to distract herself from the urge to lean towards him and start nuzzling his neck.

"Well, as I mentioned before, my mother is a history professor. She threw my father out when I was only three, so I don't really remember much about him. My mom raised me all by herself, so it has pretty much just been the two of us. Until a few years ago, anyway. She met a great guy when I was at college. It took some adjusting to the idea of a step-dad, but I like him and its nice seeing Mom being able to enjoy some luxury. She worked too hard for so long providing for the two of us."

"I'm sorry," Caley said.

"Why? It's not your fault. He was abusive, and I'm proud of her for sticking up for herself and me. It's part of the reason I decided to become a cop. To protect those who can't protect themselves." Caley nodded, another puzzle piece falling into place. It explained why he was so respectful and why he defended Sven for protecting the picker girl.

"So where is home when you're not backpacking?" Owen asked. Caley hesitated, unsure if she could tell him the truth but was saved by a set of bright headlights coming up the drive. Once again, Owen opened her door, waiting for her to settle herself before closing it, and going around to enter from the other side. The cab driver was the same man who dropped them off and on the drive down the hill back to town they chatted about the food and the wine. The driver was looking for a place to take his wife for their wedding anniversary, and Caley and Owen both agreed that he could do no wrong choosing the Apple and Grape.

The cab pulled to a stop outside the police station, Owen handing over the payment with a generous tip. "Have a good night you two," the cabbie wished them warmly. Smiling at Owen, Caley thought that they already were. She couldn't remember a better one.

"I just need to go inside and grab my keys off the front desk; otherwise I won't be able to get into my apartment," Owen said. "Do you want to come in?" When she hesitated, he blushed. Misinterpreting her reluctance, he clarified, "I meant the police station, not my apartment." Then he added awkwardly, "Not that you're not welcome in my apartment."

In actual fact, it had been the idea of entering the station which had made Caley pause. Police stations tended to freak her out. But Owen's reaction made her laugh and taking a firmer grip on his hand, she answered, "Sure," hoping that he didn't sense her fear.

Owen pulled open the large glass door before ushering Caley through. The inside was much like all the other police stations she had seen, with its smell of ink, paper, sweat, and disinfectant. Behind the desk to the left, Mike sat, eyes glazed from looking at a computer for too long. Looking up, he broke into a wide grin. "Well, hello. Its looks like you two have had a good night," he said warmly. Caley couldn't help it anxiously looking down at her dress to see if there was any evidence of their laying in the grass. She couldn't see anything but still struggled to meet

Mike's teasing gaze sure that her face was giving away their story.

"Just popping in to get my keys," Owen said. Mike opened his desk drawer and pulled out a ring of keys, handing them to Owen.

"Here you go. Also, Captain wants to talk to you about," Mike's eyes glanced in Caley's direction, "the current investigation. There's been an update. It shouldn't take long."

"Would you mind waiting in the staff room for me?" Owen asked. "Then I can walk you home."

"Sure," Caley said, trying to ignore the fact that her heart had started beating faster. He led her down a corridor and turned into the first door on the right. The staff room had a sink, fridge, cupboards, and counter against one wall allowing the on-duty officers to prepare their meals. The rest of the room held a handful of four-seater tables and chairs, plus two couches.

"If you want tea, there are bags and sugar next to the kettle and milk in the fridge. I'll be as quick as I can," Owen said, giving her a light kiss on the lips before turning to leave. Walking to the counter, Caley turned the kettle on. Opening the cupboards below the sink, she found the mugs. Adding a tea bag and a spoonful of sugar Caley poured in a dash of milk from the carton in the fridge. Once the kettle had finished boiling, she filled her mug, leaving the tea bag in to brew. Turning, Caley tried to decide where to sit. As her eyes skimmed the room, she noticed the opposite wall. The sight made her freeze. She'd barely noticed the bulletin board when she'd entered. It was covered with images of missing persons.

There were dozens of them, mostly women. Staring out at her from the center was Hannah. Her eyes seeming to bore into Caley, causing her dream from the night before to come rushing back. She was so startled, the sight so unexpected, that she didn't notice the mug sliding from her fingers until it was too late. With a crash it shattered into a dozen pieces, taking Caley's peace of mind with it.

CHAPTER 9

"Caley, are you alright?" Owen came into the room, alerted by the sounds of the mug shattering. Entering the staff room, he found her crouched on the floor, trying to pick up the shards of porcelain with her bare hands. She was shaking badly, her hands trembling so much that one of the larger pieces cut her finger as she tried to pick it up.

"Leave it. I'll grab the dustpan," Owen said. Opening a cupboard to the right of the sink, Owen pulled out a blue plastic dustpan and brush. Coming back, gently moving her still trembling hands out of the way, he swept up the shattered remains of the mug. "What happened?"

Instead of answering him, Caley simply pointed at the missing person's board. "Oh, Caley, I should have warned you. I should have thought. I'm sorry," Owen said, wrapping an arm around her. In response she wrapped her own arms around his neck, clinging to him. She sobbed silently, tears running down her cheeks. He stroked her hair, wondering at her having such a strong reaction. Yes,

MIRANDA HARVEY & & CATE ALEXANDER

the number of women who had gone missing over the past months was frightening, but she seemed stronger than this. Perhaps it was the wine? Or maybe, during her travels, she had met one of the girls? Recognized one of them?

"Do you know any of them?" Owen asked in a gentle voice. The way she suddenly stiffened in his arms, he thought her answer was going to be yes. Instead, she just shook her head. Yet something had definitely frightened her. Half carrying her, he led her to the couch and sat down next to her. He waited patiently as her tears subsided, and she got herself under control.

"I'm sorry, it was just a shock," she mumbled. "I guess I'm tired, it's been a long day." Owen nodded, that could explain her reaction. He had been an idiot, forgetting that of course, she had worked that day. No wonder she was tired.

"You have nothing to worry about," Owen said soothingly, indicating the bulletin board. "No one has gone missing from around here. We've just been tasked with watching out in case any locals know anything about it. That's actually what my boss wanted to talk to me about."

"Has one of the girls been found?" Caley asked, hopefully.

"I don't know. The Captain was about to tell me when you dropped the cup. If I make you another cup of tea, do you think you could wait a little longer? You can wait in the corridor if you want where the posters won't disturb you?" he asked, hesitant to leave her but also knowing that duty called. There had been a slump to the Captain's shoulders that didn't bode well, but he didn't want to tell Caley that and scare her further.

With a shake of her head and then, slightly trembling, a straightening of her shoulders, Caley sat up. "No, I'll be alright. I can wait. But maybe let's not risk another cup of tea," she said with a slight smile.

"If you're sure?"

"I'm sure. The sooner you go, the sooner you come back, right?" Owen nodded, smiling, reassured by the fact she had stopped trembling.

"I'll be back as soon as I can."

Caley waited until she could no longer hear the clicking of Owen's footsteps on the concrete floor of the corridor, signaling that he had reached the linoleum of the entry hall. Then she crept to the staff room door and twisted the bolt, so it locked. If someone tried to enter, it would buy her the time needed to change form. She would just have to try and think of some excuse, but she guessed she would hear them before they got close. At least that was the plan.

She had never tried a partial change before, never had the need until now. But she had to find out what the Captain wanted to tell Owen. She didn't think Owen had lied when he said that there were no missing persons from the area, but she had sensed a half-truth. As someone who had to be evasive with her answers almost daily, she could tell when someone wasn't completely honest. But her human ears weren't cut out for eaves-dropping from a distance. A wolf form would work, but a fox would be better. Sitting on the couch, crossing her legs, she rested her hands, one on top of the other, in her lap. She closed her eyes. She thought of the Fennec fox she'd seen once in a zoo, with its large ears and exceptional hearing. She concentrated on just the shape of its ears, the sharply pointed snout, the small inquisitive eyes. At the same time, she tried to balance it with the feel of her human hands, weaving her fingers together, trying to keep them human. It was hard work, and sweat began to bead on her forehead. Twice she lost her concentration when she heard the buzz of the station door opening followed by the ring of a phone, making her want to growl in frustration.

Then she had it. The world became a symphony of sound so suddenly that she was lost in the noise for a moment. Taking a deep breath, she tried to separate the sounds from one another. She ignored the click of Mike's fingers on his keyboard, the whir of the heater and the tapping of a frustrated visitor's finger against the wood of a desk. She listened for Owen's voice and found it, muffled only slightly by the closed door of the Captain's office.

"Where was she found?" Owen asked, his voice sounding sad and tired, more tired than it had when he'd been in the room with her minutes before.

"In an abandoned van parked at one of the lookout spots at Lake Ann. About twenty miles from here. The plates had been removed, and the car's VIN number scratched out," a voice deep voice answered. She assumed it was the Captain's, and he sounded as tired as Owen, as tired as Caley suddenly felt.

"That's getting closer to us. And the signs point to the same person?" Owen asked.

"I'm afraid so. The girl's head was shaved, her teeth pulled, her finger and toenails removed, and her blood was drained. There was barely enough left for her poor parents to be able to identify her."

"Shit," Owen swore. "Someone needs to catch this sicko."

"Agreed. But for now, the Commissioner just wants us to be alert. To question any strangers coming into town. I don't suppose your girl knows anything?"

Caley couldn't stop the flush of pleasure she felt at the Captain's words, but her stomach sunk as Owen replied, "No, Caley doesn't know anything. I've already asked her if she recognizes any of the victims." Her fox ears picked up the doubt in his tone that her human hearing had not heard. Owen suspected that she was lying to him.

"Hmmm, well, I think we need to come up with a plan to canvas the area. Maybe put out a reward for anyone with information? The more eyes we have on this, the better."

"Agreed, Sir."

"But not tonight. You go see your young lady home, and we'll discuss it in the morning, Sergeant."

"Thanks, Sir." Caley heard the sound of the Captain's office door creak open. Hurriedly she tried to think herself human, her head changing so fast from fox to woman that for one horrible second, she thought she'd gone deaf. But it was only the comparison of her human hearing, so weak after the Fennec fox's superior sense. At the last moment, she remembered the locked door and just managed to unbolt it as Owen turned the handle. He looked a little surprised to find her standing there but said nothing.

On the walk home, they were both subdued, heads filled with thoughts of other things. Owen held her hand, and every now and then would give it a squeeze as if reassuring himself that she was still there. That she was alright. Caley kept thinking about Hannah, how happy and innocent the girl looked in the photograph with her horse. She wondered if the girl really had been an equine shifter like Artemis said, then tried to laugh off the thought, trying to convince herself that the events of the night before were still no more than a dream.

When they reached The Last Drop, Owen pulled her to a stop and then against him in a tight embrace. She hugged him back, both saying nothing as they enjoyed the comfort of the others' arms. He kissed the top of her head, sending a shiver down her spine, before leaning back and looking her straight in the eyes,

"Are you sure you're alright?" he asked.

"Yes. I was just tired. I need some sleep," Caley reassured him, hoping he wouldn't ask any more questions about if she knew the girl.

He didn't, instead saying, "That's good. I'm sorry, but I won't be able to see you for a few days. The Captain's given me a lot of work to do, and I won't have much downtime." Her face fell slightly at his words, surprised at how much she was already looking forward to seeing him again even though she knew she shouldn't be. "But it won't be for too long. Can I have your number? I can call you or text you?"

"I don't have a cell phone," Caley admitted. "But I am sure if you call here Melody will put you through."

"Sure," he said, looking at her a little oddly. She knew it was rare for someone of their age not to have a cell, but Felix had once told her how easily they could be traced. So now she made do with the rare payphone she could find. It wasn't as if Caley had anyone to call anyway, at least not until now. To distract him, she reached up and kissed him. It wasn't as passionate a kiss as it had been in the vineyard, but it also wasn't as gentle as their first. Her mouth was becoming familiar with his, learning the way his lips curved, the feel of them against hers. Their tongues dancing in a way that no longer had the awkwardness of a first kiss. A kiss that was both a hello and a goodbye.

When they eventually pulled apart, she was a little breathless. "Thank you for tonight Owen, it was the best night I've had in ages," she said, meaning it.

"Until next time," he said, kissing her cheek before walking away. Caley watched him walk to the corner of the road, waving as he turned back to look for her. Then she pulled open the heavy door and headed inside. It was late, and there were only two customers, both perched on the stools by the bar. Melody waved at her from behind the counter, but Caley didn't feel like talking. Instead, she waved back and headed for the stand near the door to the accommodation levels, the one that held tourist brochures and maps. She searched until she found the map she needed, the one that would show her how to get to Lake Ann.

CHAPTER 10

Caley sat on the bed in her room, legs crossed, with the map of Michigan spread out before her. If she followed the roads, it was just over 15 miles to Lake Ann, less if she took shortcuts and didn't get lost. In wolf form, Caley could cover 25 miles running at full tilt. Considering that the terrain would be strange, she allowed herself two hours. Then another two to find the crime scene and discover what she could. That meant a six-hour round trip at the very least. Looking at her watch, she saw it was almost 1am. Yawning, she considered her options. There was no way she could leave tonight and be back in time for her shift. Plus, after her restless night, she was already struggling to focus and knew she would need all her senses working at full capacity. Her body begged for a couple of days rest, but the longer she left the scene, the harder it would be to find anything useful, anything that the cops hadn't already noticed. Folding the map carefully, she inserted it into her backpack and crawled into bed. Good night's sleep or not, she would go as soon as it got dark the following night.

Half expecting she would struggle to fall asleep, she was surprised when her internal clock woke her in the morning in plenty of time to get ready for her shift. She felt rested with no memory of any dreams. Certainly none of a golden goddess anyway. The daylight diluted her fears, but not her resolve to find out more. Daniel and Melody both peppered her with questions when she came downstairs, wanting to know all the details of her date with Owen. They oohed and ahhed when she told them about the food and the dancing. The star gazing among the vines she kept as their own special secret. Her shift passed quickly. Caley found that after three days she was already settling into a routine. The regulars already greeted her by name, and more than one asked about Owen. News traveled fast in a small town. She tried not to be too obvious by looking too often at her watch or the clock on the wall, calculating the hours until she could leave, but Melody noticed.

"You got another date tonight?" she asked with a suggestive smile.

Unable to think of a better lie, Caley simply nodded. At least the excuse would explain why she wasn't in her room if anyone came looking for her. When her shift finished, Caley hung up her apron and, with great effort, managed not to sprint up the stairs. Locking her bedroom door behind her, she pulled her pack from its hiding place and emptied out the contents. Traveling light was a must. Her toiletries and spare clothes could remain behind, but she added the dog collar and tag just in case. Her palm-sized mag light would come in handy. However, she couldn't decide if she should take her small first aid kit. The map, even folded, was bulky. The wind was picking up, it would likely blow away if she tried to look at it in the open. Instead, she grabbed the cardboard coaster from her side table and a pen she had borrowed from Melody. In tiny handwriting, being as neat as she could, she wrote out the directions for the route she had chosen. Hopefully, she wouldn't need it, but it made her feel better knowing that she had it just in case. She took off her watch and placed it in her pack with the coaster, deciding to add the first aid kit at the last minute. Better safe than sorry. The last item to go into the backpack was her room key. Zipping it up she lifted it, assessing its weight. It was a little heavier than she had hoped, but it would have to do.

Looking around for somewhere to store her wallet and family photograph, her most valuable possessions, her eyes fell on her pillow. Lifting and turning it so that she could slide the items into the back, she gasped when she spotted the arrowhead. Dropping the pillow, she picked up the arrowhead, examining it, turning it over in her hands. It looked to be made out of metal, polished so smooth that it almost slipped from her fingers. The point was razor-sharp; she sliced the tip of one finger so quickly that at first she didn't realize, not until it started to throb and blood began to drip onto the bedsheets.

"Shit," she muttered, opening her pack and removing the first aid kit to pull out a bandage. As she applied it to her finger, she stared at the arrowhead which lay inno- cently in the middle of the bed where she had dropped it. If the arrowhead was real, which the cut on her finger proved if nothing else, then that meant that the dream had been real. That there were others like her and that they were in danger. With this realization, her determination to investigate the crime scene grew. Carefully picking up the arrowhead, she stuffed it with the other items into the pillow and placed it back into position at the top of her bed.

She changed out of her work clothes into a fresh pair of jeans, a clean t-shirt, her sweatshirt and finally a hoodie. It felt a little bulky, but it was going to be cold out by the lake tonight. Then, adding to the impression that she was going out on a date, she took the time to put on a little makeup and brush her hair. Glancing out of her bedroom window, she was glad to see that the sun had set. In two nights it would be a full moon. Moonlight streamed through the window, both a blessing and a problem. The light would make it easier for her to see once she reached the woods, but it would also make it easier for others to spot her. A lone wolf running around town was bound to draw unwanted attention. Glad she had chosen to pack the collar she decided to start the journey in dog form then switch once she was hidden in the shadows of the forest.

Heading down the stairs, she waved to Melody who was busy serving customers. Grateful she wouldn't need to stop and chat she hastily left the bar. Outside she made her way to the dumpster area. Slipping between the gates and placing her pack on the ground, handles facing up, the collar beside it, she crouched down on her hands and knees, careful not to kneel in anything gross. Clearing her mind, she focused on the image of the black Labrador that had hung around Bad Betty's Barbecue. She thought of his lolling tongue, the way he had slanted his head to the side when listening to her, his excitement when she'd left him a plate of scrapped steak. She felt the magic start to flow from her core through her body as one by one each part of her shifted form. Opening her eyes, now able to make out fine details in the dark, she sniffed the air, adrenalin starting to course through her.

The journey to Lake Ann had been surprisingly easy, and she had made good time. It seemed there wasn't much traffic on the roads on a Sunday night and she had managed to stay in wolf form for most of the way. She guessed it had taken a little over an hour but hadn't bothered going through the hassle of checking her watch. What she hadn't reckoned with was how difficult it was going to be to find the actual crime scene. The police captain had mentioned a lookout, and she'd been confident there would be a tourist sign with all the lookouts mapped out. She had been right about that. What she hadn't foreseen was that the lake featured over twenty lookout spots. With the rolling terrain and curving edges, it had taken her much longer to find the right one. It also didn't help that her wolf nose kept getting distracted by other enticing smells.

In fact, she would have gone right past it if not for the bright yellow police tape. Rather than parking the van in the lookout parking lot, the driver had taken it off-road, undoubtedly hoping to use the scrub bushes and trees as a shield. The van was a dark blue with its license plates removed, so there was little to reflect the moonlight. She approached it cautiously, ears twitching trying to catch any sound that indicated someone was about. But all she picked up were night calls of nocturnal birds and animals which inhabited the lake, the slosh of the water and the whisper of the trees. Ducking beneath the yellow plastic tape, she made her way carefully towards the vehicle, scanning the ground for footprints. She made out four unique sets of human footprints but couldn't tell if they belonged to the police or to the hunter.

Reaching the van, she quickly realized that she needed to change form. There was no way that she would be able to open the van's door, or even peer through the darkened windows as a wolf. Too frightened to change out in the open she moved so that she could squat behind a cluster of bushes and began the slow process of changing back into her human form. While she waited for her human eyes to adjust to the dark, she suddenly became aware of how cold it was, the wind off the lake, making her blood freeze. She missed her wolf form's thick winter coat. She thought about seeing if she could conjure it by itself like she had with the ears of the fox but then decided against it. If it back-fired, she would be vulnerable. Pulling her watch out of her backpack, she checked the time. She had left The Last Drop almost four hours ago. If she wanted to make it back before daylight, she would need to hurry.

Pulling the mag light out of her pack and switching it on, she shielded the top of the bulb with her cupped hand. Pointing it at the rear doors, she could make out a fine residue. Fingerprint dust? Pulling the sleeve of her hoodie down so that it covered her hand, she slowly pulled the handle. She expected it would be locked, but luck must have been on her side because the handle turned without a fuss, and the door swung open. Perhaps the police had needed to jimmy it open and hadn't been able to re-lock it? What she saw inside made her gasp, and the contents of her stomach heave as nausea overwhelmed her. She sprinted to the bushes just in time, emptying the remains of her lunch into the sand. She cursed herself for not thinking to bring a bottle of water. Or anything that she could use to wash the taste in her mouth away. Pulling everything out of her bag, she searched for the stick of gum that usually floated around at the bottom. Finding it, she quickly undid the wrapper and shoved it into her mouth.

But the sight of what she had seen in the van would take a lot more than water or peppermint gum to be wiped clean. The police had removed Hannah's body from the vehicle, but the floor and walls were coated in blood and vomit. With horror, Caley made out paths in the blood, made by Hannah's fingers when the poor girl must have tried to claw her way free. There were also large dents in the walls of the van and the door. She now knew why the police were unable to align the lock and the thought brought a second wave of nausea. It looked like something had thrown itself against the door - or had been thrown. In the end, the poor girl must have lost control of her bowels for the entire van stunk. Caley couldn't even contemplate the idea of going back inside. The thought of smelling all that with her wolf nose made shivers run down her spine. She had been a fool to ever think that she would do a better job than the police at finding evidence. Right at that moment, she cared less about who committed this horrific act and more about carving out as much distance between herself and the monster as she possibly could. She couldn't stay in Peregrine City, not with the killer coming closer. She needed to leave, and soon.

She hurriedly shoved her belongings back into the backpack, wanting nothing more than to run away. Realizing that in her hurry to throw up she had left the van door open she clamped a hand over her nose and mouth, and holding her breath, she tried to shut the door with her other, hoodie covered hand. She almost cried when it swung back open knowing it would take both hands to maneuver the door so it would stay shut with the busted lock. Lungs almost bursting she released her grip on her nose and slammed the door shut with all her might. Relief washed over her as it stuck in place. Struggling to move a few feet back from the van, she released the breath she had been holding in a rush. She gulped down deep mouthfuls of air, filling her lungs and letting the oxygen flood through her, too scared to breathe through her nose. Then, turning, she fled back the way she had come, waiting until she was far away before shifting back into wolf form.

CHAPTER 11

As Owen canvassed the local tourist spots, talking to the bar and restaurant owners and anyone who could have come into contact with the killer, his thoughts kept returning to Caley. He couldn't stop thinking about her and their date. He had never felt so connected, so aligned with someone before. Everything with her seemed so simple, so right. He'd been on half a dozen dates in the last year; his uniform seemed to attract most of the women in the town. But they'd always wanted something from him that he had been unwilling to give. Favors, like canceled parking tickets, or using his goodwill with most of the town's business owners to try and score perks. They'd ask him stupid questions, like if he'd ever shot anyone, and always seemed a little disappointed when his answer was no. Not Caley, she had been interested in him as a person. Wanting to know about his family and happy that he'd saved Sven. While the other women had loved to talk, Caley had preferred to listen.

As Owen's shift finished, he thought about calling into The Last Drop as he headed back to the station; to see her. He'd tried to play hard to get, telling her he couldn't see her for a few days, trying not to make it obvious how quickly he was falling for her. He already knew that her eyes would light up when he walked into the bar, drawing him to her like a moth to a flame. And he loved the way she blushed whenever he paid her a compliment like she had no idea how lovely she was. Most of all, he loved the way she smelled like snow and spring all at once, just thinking about it made his head spin. And yet he had to admit there was something strange about her too. The way she flinched at loud noises and didn't like to talk about her past. He'd met a woman whose husband had used her like a punching bag and Caley's fear almost felt like that. Almost, and yet not. Like she struggled to trust people. He hoped that one day, she would learn to trust him.

Opening the door of the police station, he saw the Captain standing near Mike's desk, talking to him. Pausing when he caught sight of Owen, the Captain said, "Ah Owen, good timing. I know that you are about to clock off, but I was hoping you wouldn't mind taking a short drive?"

Owen shrugged. "I've got nothing planned, Sir. Where am I going?"

"I've just had a call from the Captain of the Lake Ann station. It turns out that the tow truck that was supposed to collect the van from the crime scene has let them down. The driver was supposed to collect it Saturday but came down with the flu and forgot to call it in. They've organized someone else to collect it, but it can't happen until tomorrow, and someone needs to check and make sure nothings tampered with. Their Captain seems to have come down with the same bug and asked if I could send someone."

"Sure thing, Sir. I can go," Owen agreed. He had to admit he was more than a little curious to check it out. From reading the police reports the killer's MO was strange. Owen didn't have much personal experience with serial killers, but he had studied case histories at the academy. Most did it for the pleasure they found in either the hunt or the kill. If it was the hunt, they tended to kill fast, if it was the kill slow. But it was strange for them to drain the victim's blood or take their hair and fingernails. Actual fingers were more common trophies.

The drive didn't take long, and the specific location set into the GPS, so he had no issue finding the exact spot. Spotting the van, still ringed by yellow police tape, he radioed in to let the Captain know. Parking the car, he positioned it so that the headlights faced the scene, bathing it in light. First, he checked the van. He knew from reading the report that the detectives had broken the lock. Pulling plastic gloves out of his pocket and putting them on, he opened the rear door. He recoiled when the smell from inside hit him like a wave and felt his stomach do a flip. Taking a few deep breaths in through his mouth, he managed to hold back the need to empty the contents of his stomach. Just. His eyes took in the blood and grime, the scratch marks, and the dents in the walls and doors. Holding one hand up against the indentation, he was surprised to find it barely spanned his palm. The coroner's report had made no mention of any broken bones, and the victim's skull was intact. Nor had they found any blood belonging to the killer. So how had the dents been made?

Closing the door again, he decided to walk the perimeter of the crime scene, to ensure no one had tampered with anything or come close. So far, the papers and news had not mentioned the discovery of Hannah's body. Hannah's devastated family were informed, but the police commander wanted to give the family time to grieve before being hounded by reporters. However, it was still possible that a local walker could have come across the site. He doubted that he would find anything, however, so he was surprised when something red caught his eye in the bushes near the lake. At first, he thought that it was trash that someone had dumped, intending to collect it and dispose of it properly. But coming closer he noticed two things. The first was the faint smell of vomit. Someone else must have had a similar reaction to his own when scenting the stench from the open van. The second was that the flash of red he had seen hadn't been from a cola can as he'd assumed but was part of the logo printed on the back of a coaster. His eyes widened as he realized that the logo was one he recognized. It was from The Last Drop. Picking it up, he turned it over and swore.

CHAPTER 12

The whole drive back to the station Owen's head had been rolling, trying to work out the meaning behind the mysteriously located coaster. He had recognized the writing instantly. There was no doubt in his mind that Caley had written it. He'd seen her neat handwriting back when she had filled in the forms for the job application at The Last Drop. But why had she written down the directions? Why had she even thought about going to the crime scene, let alone known where it was? He definitely hadn't told her nor event hinted at it, and who else would have?

Arriving back at the station he had been too befuddled to talk to Mike, brushing him off when he asked what was wrong. He'd talk to him in the morning when they went for their usual pre-work jog. For now, he needed time to think. But all night he had lain in bed, barely managing to get a wink of sleep, trying to puzzle it out in his head. How was Caley connected to the missing girl? When she had freaked out at the sight of the missing person posters, he thought she was just reacting badly because she was tired. When he'd asked her if she recognized any of the women, he had sensed something a little off in her quick denial, but again he had put it down as her just being tired. But now he was questioning it all. Was everything he thought he knew about her a lie? How was she involved?

He thought about just confronting her, asking her to tell him the truth and yet he hesitated. He knew, with every fiber of his being, that she wasn't the killer. However, try as he might, he couldn't think of why she had been at the crime scene. Perhaps a customer had asked for directions, and she hadn't actually been there at all, it was just a horrible coincidence. But he tossed that thought as quickly as it came to him. Why would she, someone new to the area, be the one to give directions. Why wouldn't the customer just have grabbed one of the maps from the tourist stand? It made no sense.

Another thing that was puzzling him was that Caley didn't own a car. It would have taken far too long to walk to the place where the killer had parked the van. If she had caught a cab, surely the driver would have reported her behavior as suspicious. He had personally talked to all the local drivers in the Peregrine City area that morning, and not one had mentioned taking a redheaded girl, or any passenger, out to Lake Ann. Something just didn't add up.

When his alarm went off the next morning, he was glad to hear it for once. Getting out of bed, he quickly put on his running gear and headed out the door to meet Mike. Jumping into his car, he drove out of town to the path which wound around Lake Michigan. Seeing the turn off to the sand dunes, they reminded him of his first date with Caley and how much fun they'd had. How excited she had been. Remembering her laugh and her smiling, happy face, he couldn't think for a moment that either belonged to a killer.

Pulling into the car park, he spotted Mike already limbering up against the wooden rails that divided the grass from the asphalt parking lot. A few feet away, a group of girls paused to watch him. Aware of their attention and enjoying it, Mike began to shadow punch the air making Owen laugh. It felt good to laugh, the sunshine and sight of his friend's antics already starting to chase away his fears. Getting out of the car, Owen stepped up next to Mike and started working on his own set of stretches. Once done they headed East along their usual course, four miles in one direction, pause for a fifteen-minute break and then run the four miles back.

Trying to talk seriously while running was difficult, so Owen decided to wait until the halfway point before voicing his concerns to Mike. Instead, he let the familiar rhythm of his feet hitting the concrete, and the beat of his heart in his ears soothe him. There was the usual group of locals out that morning, and Owen waved or nodded at most in recognition. There were the moms pushing strollers in front of them. The old couple who always held hands when they walked. The boys in wetsuits carrying their paddleboards; he admired their commitment, the autumn wind coming off the lake was freezing, a sure sign that the first winter snows weren't far away.

Reaching the halfway point, Owen sat down on one of

the benches to catch his breath, Mike taking the seat beside him. He tried to think about how to broach the subject when Mike asked, "So how did your date go?"

"It was great. Amazing actually," Owen admitted truthfully.

"Good. About time you found someone nice."

"What do you think of her?"

"Who? Caley. I think she's sweet. I don't know her as well as you do though," Mike said, nudging Owen in the ribs, "But she seems friendly enough. Why?"

"You don't think there's anything strange about her?"

"Strange? Nah. Are you getting cold feet?" Owen was about to explain about the coaster when Mike went on, "Every time you meet a girl, you have to find something wrong with her. Now you finally go on a date that you just described as amazing and it is freaking you out. Give the girl a chance."

Owen nodded; Mike was right. He needed to give Caley a chance. Needed to talk to her about the damn coaster first, give her a chance to explain. He owed her that much. Relieved to have come to a decision, he smiled at Mike, "Thanks, buddy."

"Anytime. Now I need your advice. Lisa is putting a lot of pressure on me to move in with her, but I don't think I'm ready. I mean, you've seen my place. It looks like a bomb hit it most of the time. The only time it is clean is when I know she is coming over. I'm worried if we live together, then she'll discover what a slob I truly am and dump my ass."

For the rest of their break, the two men debated whether Mike was grown up enough to move to the next step of his relationship, the discussion often causing both to break into fits of laughter startling passers-by. During the jog back to the cars, Owen found himself smiling. Everything was going to work out just fine. Caley would no doubt have a reasonable explanation, the police would catch the killer soon, and the whole matter could be put to rest. Perhaps he would pop into the bar on his way home and see if she wanted to come over to his place for dinner. Unlike Mike, Owen wasn't a slob, and he was a pretty good cook.

Waving farewell, the men split up, each to return home, shower and get into their uniforms ready to start their shifts. Opening the door to his house, Owen saw the coaster, still sitting on the sideboard where he had left it the night before. He should have handed it in, the Captain would suspend his badge if he found out he was hiding evidence. Yet, Owen hesitated. It was the one link between the crime scene and Caley, and he felt it his duty to protect her. Something about her brought out the protective instinct in him. Picking up the coaster, before he had a chance to talk himself out of it, he walked to the kitchen and, stamping on the pedal, opened the trash bin and threw the coaster in. He was already heading to his bedroom when the lid banged shut behind him.

Owen pulled into the parking lot next to Mike's Mustang, not surprised to find he'd beaten him there. Locking his car, he headed into the station. The second Owen caught sight of the look on Mike's face a wave of unease flooded through him. Something was seriously wrong. Mike looked like he had seen a ghost, and meeting Owen's gaze, he gave a twitch of his head indicating for

Owen to follow him to the staff room. Deciding that he could wait to put his personal items in his locker, Owen followed Mike down the corridor.

"Hey! You two, don't be too long. We want to go home," Gloria shouted after them. She and Thomas had done the night shift, and she sounded grumpy, impatient to leave. Ignoring her, Owen stepped through the staff room door which Mike held open, closing it behind them.

"Did you know? Is that why you asked me what I thought about her?" Mike demanded the moment the door was closed.

"Know what?" Owen asked, acting perplexed.

"This!" Mike shoved a piece of paper into Owen's hands. Looking down, he saw that it was an all-points bulletin. The date stamp across the top was from five minutes ago, it must have come through on the fax as Mike had walked in. Staring out at him from a security camera photo was the face of a woman. Even though her features were in black and white and blurred from the poor-quality camera, there was no denying that it was a photograph of Caley. In bold letters above the top of the photo were the words "Person of Interest." Below the picture were instructions that anyone with knowledge of the person's whereabouts should contact the police commissioner as soon as possible.

"Fuck," Owen swore. "I didn't know about this. Is there anything to say what she is wanted for?"

"Nope. Just this. Came through literally as I walked through the door," Mike said, confirming Owen's guess. "You're just lucky that the Captain didn't see it, or Gloria or Thomas."

"Thanks," Owen said.

"I don't know if 'thanks' is the right word, but I am guessing you want to be the one to bring her in?"

Owen nodded.

"Okay, I'll cover for you with the Captain. Tell him that you got an urgent call. But Owen," Owen looked at his friend, meeting his worried gaze, "Remember to think with your head, not your heart." It felt strange hearing Mike repeat the words Owen had so often said to him.

"I will."

"Good luck," Mike said and reaching over clasped Owen's shoulder in support. "If you need anything, let me know."

Owen left without stopping at the desk to say goodbye to Gloria, his car keys still clutched in his hand. Just shy of pulling open the station's door, he realized that taking his own car probably wasn't the smartest move. Especially if Mike's cover story involved a job. Turning, he went back to the office and walked to the key stand behind the main desk. Selecting one of the police car's keys, he replaced them on the hook with his own. Then without another glance around, he headed back out the front door. As the door closed behind him, he heard Gloria ask, "What's up with Owen? Not like him not to say hello?" It shut before he could listen to Mike's reply.

Getting in and starting the car, he'd turned off the gravel drive onto the road before the reality of what he was about to do hit him. He was about to go and take Caley into police custody. The girl he could no longer deny that he had fallen in love with. For what? An APB broadcast that had little to no information. What did a person of interest even mean? Interest in what? Was it something to do with her being at the crime scene, or was this something else entirely? There was only one way to find out and pushing down the accelerator he headed in the direction of The Last Drop.

CHAPTER 13

Grateful that it was Tuesday and her day off Caley looked at the list in her hands. It wasn't a long list, just the bare necessities she would need until she reached the next town. Her bags were already packed, ready for her to return. Looking out in the morning light, she could already see the moon hanging in the bright blue sky. Tonight would be a full moon, perfect for traveling through the woods.

Her only regrets were lying to Melody and not getting to say goodbye to Owen. After the horrific crime scene, she had wanted nothing more than to run to him, to have him hold her, to feel safe even for a moment. But she couldn't. Doing so would only put him in danger, and she wouldn't do that. It would break her heart to leave him. She had never before felt such a powerful connection to anyone, never had someone seem to see her truth beneath all the lies, not like he did. She considered leaving a note for him, but what would she write, "Killer after me. Have to leave. BTW I love you." It was better that she just leave and have him think she didn't care, even if it was tearing her in two. If she saw him again, she would have to keep him at arms' length, somehow.

Grabbing her purse, she headed down the stairs, her mind lost in the list of things she needed to buy. As she reached the bottom of the stairs, she was so deep in her own thoughts that she didn't notice Owen. But when he called out her name, in a tone so serious for a moment she didn't recognize it, she looked up and felt her face flush. Before she could stop it, her face broke into a warm grin at the sight of him, a smile which he did not return. Looking closer, she noticed how rigid he was standing and that there was no trace of the usual kindness she found in his eyes.

"Owen?" she asked hesitantly.

"We need to talk. Come with me," Owen said, striding towards her, and taking a firm but gentle hold of her arm, he led her outside. As the door started to swing shut behind them, she caught Melody's eye, but the bar manager looking as puzzled by this turn of events as she did.

"Owen, what's wrong?" Caley asked, starting to feel a little frightened. In her mind, she ran through the events of their dinner date. Nothing had happened that would cause him to suddenly act so strange. When he had left her two nights ago, he'd kissed her and made plans for their next date together. Was he somehow sensing her intention to leave?

Owen didn't let go of her arm until they reached the place where he had parked the police car. Turning her so that she faced him, he fumbled in his pants' pocket and pulled out a piece of cardboard. He held it up so she could see it, and Caley felt her blood run cold. Dread settled like a stone in her stomach. It was the coaster she had taken from the bar to write the directions on. In her fluster the night before, she must have dropped it without realizing.

"I found this at Lake Ann. I know this is your handwriting, don't try and deny it. What were you doing there?" Owen asked in a calm voice, totally contradicting the emotions flickering in his eyes. Disappointment, fear, hurt, and something else she couldn't read. She wanted to lie to him but knew that he would see right through it, and it would only make the situation worse.

Instead, she said the only thing she could think of, "I can't tell you, Owen. I'm so sorry. But I didn't kill that girl, I promise you that."

At her words, the tension in Owen's body seemed to relax though it didn't alter the way he was looking at her. "And why are the police looking for you? What mess are you involved in?" Her eyes widened in surprise at his questions. The police were looking for her? This was news to her.

"You didn't know," he said, his voice softening slightly. "We received an APB bulletin this morning listing you as a person of interest. I'm here to take you in."

"You can't!" Caley exclaimed so loudly it was almost a shout. A couple, walking their dog, paused to look at them before hurrying on after Owen directed a scowl in their direction.

"I have to. It's my job. I have to. Unless you can tell me why I shouldn't?"

Caley shook her head, and her body started to tremble.

She should have left yesterday, despite how tired she had felt, despite not having the supplies she needed. Just grabbed her stuff and run. Her eyes darted around, looking for a way to make an escape even though she knew it was too late. As if sensing her desire to run, Owen took hold of one of her hands, half comforting, half holding her in place.

"If you don't tell me what is wrong, Caley, I can't help you," Owen pleaded, letting go of his professional demeanor. This time looking into his eyes, she saw that the fear and disappointment was gone. The hurt was still there, but it had made room for another feeling, and for a moment, it surprised her, making her catch her breath. The emotion in Owen's dark brown eyes was love. He honestly was offering to help her, to protect her because he was in love with her. And the realization made her heart swell but also shatter. Because how could she tell him the truth and have him believe her. How quickly would that love turn back to fear if he found out what she was, that she was a freak of nature?

At her silence, Owen shook his head, "So be it," he muttered, pulling open the back door of the police car. "I'm hoping that I won't have to cuff you to get you to come with me?" he asked, his voice quiet, all the fight and passion having been drained out of him by her silence.

"Owen, you can't take me in. Please," she begged.

"I don't have a choice, Caley. Please don't make me cuff you," he said softly, voice shaking with emotion. Looking at him, she knew she didn't have a choice. Not really. If she ran, he would only chase her and force her to go, and it would break anything that was ever possible between them. Silently, trying to hold back the tears that threatened to fall, she bent her head and slipped into the back seat. Owen closed the door behind her. The click as he activated the lock sounded like a shot, killing any chance of escape and sealing the fate which awaited her. No longer able to stop the tears from falling, she was grateful he hadn't decided to handcuff her after all as she tried to stop the flood with her hands. As Owen got into the driver's seat, their eyes met in the rear-view mirror. He looked like he was about to say something then stopped, his lips thinning as if trying to hold back the words. Reaching across, Owen opened the glove compartment and pulled out a tissue. Without a word, he passed it to her through the bars which separated them.

Caley couldn't decide which was more overwhelming, her fear of what was waiting for her at the police station or her sense of loss at losing Owen. Living a life on the run, she had already had to give up so much. Her family, childhood friends, and those few she'd made along the way, even her chance of a normal life. But this, this seemed like one thing too many. What was the point of running, of saving her life if there was nothing worth living for? She may as well face her demons and be done with it. She was done running.

The decision cleared Caley's mind, and immediately she knew what she had to do. She thought of the dogs that had run to them in the park the first time she had walked together. Closing her eyes, she held a picture of one, a golden retriever, in her mind and let her magic flow through her. As it moved from her core to her heart and along her limbs, she gave in to it, letting it wash away her anxiety and fear. Whatever happened next was ultimately out of her control. She was putting her fate and her heart in Owen's hands.

Once the shift was complete, she opened her eyes. It was strange looking at the back of a car from a dog's perspective. For one thing, her head was a lot lower, and she had to stretch, sitting up on her hind legs, to see over the partition. Looking into the rear-view mirror, hoping to catch Owen's eye, she saw that he was focused entirely on the view in front of him, a crease of concentration across his forehead a sure sign that he was fighting an urge to keep himself from looking at her.

Unable to think of anything else, she did the one thing most dogs do to get someone's attention. She barked.

CHAPTER 14

The sound of a loud bark made Owen jump. It was coming from his back seat. How the hell had that happened? Looking up into his rear-view mirror, he caught sight of the golden retriever sitting quietly in the middle of the passenger seat. His eyes widened in shock, his jaw dropped open, and without thinking, he slammed his foot on the brake. The sudden stop made the unrestrained dog shoot forward, its furry body crashing into the partition. It let out a whimper of pain. Behind him, another driver was also forced to slam on his brakes, and from the way he was screaming obscenities at him, Owen guessed he'd come within a hair's breadth of ramming into the back of them. But Owen wasn't really concerned about the other driver. Instead, his eyes darted around the back seat, looking for any sign of Caley.

The dog barked a second time and, again, it made him jump. The driver behind them started beeping his horn. Looking around, Owen noticed an empty car bay in front of the Black Market coffee shop and hurriedly pulled the car off to the side of the road. The infuriated driver scowled darkly at Owen as he drove past. If Owen hadn't been driving a police car, he was sure the aggravated driver would have done far worse. The guy would likely report him to the Captain for reckless driving, but right at that moment, it was the least of his worries.

Holding up his hands in the universal sign for stay, Owen opened his door and climbed awkwardly out of the car, not losing sight of the dog for a second. Reaching the passenger door on the driver's side, he tried the handle and found it locked. Quickly racing around the back of the car Owen tried the handle on the side which he'd opened for Caley to get in. Again, he found it locked. He could almost feel the wheels turning inside his head, trying to figure out a rational explanation for what was happening. How had Caley managed not only switch places with a dog but to do so while the car was moving and both passenger doors were locked?

Owen looked around as if searching for something, he didn't know what for, just something. Perhaps for someone to come and explain to him what the hell was going on. But, of course, no one did. All he saw was the intrigued gaze of the customers in the coffee shop trying to work out what all the fuss was about. Turning back, he looked at the dog who was still sitting calmly on the back seat of his car. It wore no collar, but apart from that there was nothing unusual about it, in fact, it looked somehow familiar. He tried to remember where he had seen the dog before, but the memory escaped him. On impulse, he placed his hand flat against the window, trying to see if he could make it slide down. It didn't budge. But the dog, looking him straight in the eyes, lifted one paw and a placed it so it aligned with his hand on the opposite side of the glass. The second he pulled his hand away, the dog dropped its paw. Strange. Nervously he ran his hand through his hair and watched, astounded, as the dog mimicked his action, brushing its own paw over its head. Again, the moment he lowered his hand, so did the dog.

Owen tilted his head to the left, the dog did the same. Owen winked his right eye, and again, the dog mirrored him. Following a strange compulsion, Owen clapped his hands once. The dog, sitting back on its haunches, tapped its two front paws together. This by itself would have astonished him, but as the dog changed position, he real-ized something else. Something that made him think that he was starting to lose his mind. Because in a flash he remembered the dog that had greeted them in the park the first day he and Caley had walked together. That dog was a male. But this dog, almost an exact match, was female.

Feeling like a complete fool, Owen asked in a soft voice, "Can you understand me?" The dog gave a quick nod. Then, his voice quavering, he asked, "Caley?" The dog's response was three quick nods of its head. Owen couldn't help it, he instinctively stepped away from the car. Putting distance between him and this strange animal that was freaking him the fuck out, sure that he must have hit his head. Perhaps the car behind them had actually smashed into them, and Owen was currently lying in the hospital, in a coma, having the strangest dream of his life. As he stepped away, the dog let out a whine, a sound so full of sorrow that it made him stop, and as he watched a single tear slid from the corner of its eye down its muzzle. And Owen knew that with that one teardrop, whether or not it was indeed a dream, stepping away wasn't an option. Because looking into the dog's emerald green eyes, he didn't see a golden retriever anymore. He saw Caley.

Owen still had absolutely no idea what he was supposed to do next. The only thing he was sure of was that he couldn't return to the station. If Owen tried to explain to the Captain that the dog in the backseat of his car was actually Caley, they would be sure to throw him in the loony bin. Getting back into the car and starting the engine, he looked at the dog, at Caley, in the rear-view mirror.

"What am I supposed to do now?" he asked. Nudging his neck with her cold nose, as if ensure his attention, the dog moved to the other side of the back seat. Lifting a paw, she tapped the top left corner of the window.

"I don't understand," he said puzzled. The dog tapped again and gave a little yip. Communicating with a dog was hard. She touched the window again, this time moving her paw in a small circle encompassing the top left corner of the window. This time he saw it.

"You want to go to the woods?" he asked. She gave a happy yip and smiled a doggy smile at him.

"Alright then," Owen said, switching on the car's indicator. As he pulled out of the parking spot, he still wasn't sure if he was dreaming.

Pulling the car off the road and parking it at the side of the woods, Owen got out and unlocking it opened the rear passenger door. The dog bounded out and then sat patiently, waiting for Owen to lock the car. With a twitch of her ears, the dog indicated the woods and then walked off, checking over her shoulder as if to make sure that Owen was following. Owen followed, wondering where the hell she was leading him. Passing a sign reminding walkers to keep their dogs on the leash, he let out a laugh making the dog jump. "Serves her right after the scare she gave me," Owen thought, feeling a little better. He just prayed that there weren't any rangers on duty to catch them.

They'd been walking for about twenty minutes when the dog stopped, sniffing the air and looking around. They were surrounded by trees, the only sounds that of birds calling to each other and the breeze as it rifled the leaves. Turning to face Owen, the dog held up one paw, mimicking his motion of stay from earlier. He stopped and waited. At first, nothing happened, the dog just seemed to sit there. But then he felt it. A subtle change in the air pressure and the feeling of being both hot and cold all at once. The air seemed to shimmer, and his vision of the dog blurred. Then he blinked his eyes and where the dog had sat but a second before was Caley, sitting cross-legged and dressed in the same clothes she'd been wearing when he had picked her up that morning.

Suddenly Owen felt the urgent need to sit. Not caring what lay on the ground beneath him; he plonked down, landing hard on his butt. But he didn't mind the pain, in all this craziness it was the one thing that felt real.

"I'm so sorry, Owen. I was just so scared to tell you, and I was pretty sure that you wouldn't have believed me anyway," Caley said, voice shy. She wouldn't meet his gaze, staring at her fingers as if afraid of how he was going to react. He wondered suddenly how many other people knew her secret and if any of them had responded poorly. Plus, he had to admit that she was right, there was no way he would have believed her.

So many questions were jumping through his mind, but he asked the most obvious one first, "How?"

"I don't really know. I was fourteen when I changed the first time in my sleep. Scared the hell out me and my parents freaked. Instead of their daughter, they woke in the morning to find a wolf in her bed. My dad almost shot me," Caley said, frowning at the memory. "It took me over a week to discover how to change back, and by then, there were search parties out looking for me."

Owen tried to imagine it. How she must have felt, how terrified she must have been, and he felt his fear start to wash away. "A wolf?" he asked.

"Yeah. I can turn into a wolf or a dog or a fox. I've tried to turn into a cat, but that didn't work so I guess it's just anything in the canine family."

"And you can control it? When you change?"

"I can now but I couldn't at first. It would happen when I was asleep or if I was scared. My parents didn't know what to do. They wanted to help me, but they had no idea how. They were also scared that I would turn on them, or that I'd hurt my brother or sister. They started locking me in my room at night, they stopped me going to school, it was awful," Caley said, breaking into a sob. "You have no idea how hard it is to see your own parents look at you with fear in their eyes. Be afraid to touch you.

Matthew and Emily never seemed afraid, but my parents wouldn't let them near me." She was crying hard now, the sobs wracking her body as she struggled to get the words out.

Crawling towards her, Owen wrapped Caley in a tight embrace, unsure what else to do or say to comfort her. She continued to cry, her tears drenching his shirt, but he didn't care. He would hold her for as long as was needed. He wasn't afraid of her, his heart breaking for the girl she had been.

Slowly as the minutes passed, her tears slowed and then stopped. Pulling back, she looked up at him, her emerald green eyes still wet from unshed tears, "You're not scared of me?"

"No," he answered truthfully.

"I've been alone for so long since I ran away. I've had to keep this secret for so long," Caley said, gulping to swallow the last tears. "But someone knows. Someone is hunting me, Owen, and I am so scared."

"Hush now, sweetheart. It's going to be alright. No one is going to hurt you, I promise. You're not alone anymore. You have me," he said, lowering his head, tasting the saltiness of her tears as he kissed her gently on the mouth, sealing his promise.

CHAPTER 15

Caley had to admit it felt a little odd to be sitting in the front seat of a police car. Strange, but far better than sitting in the back. Owen held the steering wheel with one hand, holding tightly to her hand with the other. He hadn't let go of her since she had told him her story. He also hadn't told her where they were going, just asked her to trust him and she did. It felt wonderful to let someone else make the decisions like a weight had been lifted off her shoulders.

They drove for almost an hour, not saying much. Owen still had that look on his face. The look showing that his mind was working at a million miles an hour and she didn't want to interrupt. Instead, she sat back in the seat and looked out the window. They had quickly passed out of the town, up the hill past the Apple and Grape. But Owen didn't slow the car, continuing on until they reached the crest of that hill and then the next one. The stress of the past few days, combined with her lack of sleep, finally got the better of her. Feeling safe as well as exhausted, Caley fell asleep.

She woke when the car's wheels hit a gravel road, the unfamiliar sound jerking her awake, and saw that they were turning off onto a drive arched by tall pine trees. A wooden picket fence marked the property and the mail-box, standing at an odd angle, read number 6. The yard was filled with tall grasses that looked to be waist high at least. At the end of the drive, a wooden house came into view, old fashioned but not run down and clearly well-loved. Caley wondered who lived there. She looked around for another car but could not see one, assuming if the owner was home, the vehicle must be parked around the back. Pulling the police car to a stop by the house's porch Owen turned to her, "I know it doesn't look like much, but you'll be safe here, at least until we think of a better solution."

"Who lives here?"

"No one, or at least not right now. My mom and step-dad have it as a holiday home, but they won't use for it for a while. They came for the cherry season so they won't be back for at least six months. Your nearest neighbor is half a mile on either side, so you'll have privacy in case you want to turn into a wolf or something." Caley marveled at the way he mentioned her shifting so matter-of-factly like he was already used to the idea.

Getting out of the car, Owen directed her to wait by the front door. Standing there, she watched him walk to where a woodpile was stacked neat and tidy, and rummage around. Finding what he wanted he pulled a log from the pile and to Caley's surprise, she heard a click and then a piece of the top of the wood released and slid loose. Removing the key hidden inside Owen pushed the cover back into place and returned the fake log back into its hiding place. With a grin, he came back to her and opened the front door.

The house had a slight musky smell but apart from that was neat and tidy. Going to each of the front windows Owen pulled opened the blinds and then released the latches, opening the windows to let the fresh air in.

"It shouldn't take too long to air the place out. How about I do the rest of the setting up, and you look around?"

Leaving him to it, Caley opened the first of three doors leading off the main room and found the master bedroom. The large bed neatly made; a hand-knitted patchwork blanket draped over the cream quilt cover. The second door led into the bathroom, and Caley almost groaned when she caught sight of the deep tub. It had been so long since she had been able to have a relaxing soak. The types of accommodation that fit into her limited budget rarely afforded the luxury of a bathtub. The final door opened onto what she guessed was Owen's mother's craft room. A white sewing machine sat in the middle of a table surrounded by clothing patterns and scraps of material. There was also a bookshelf double stacked with hardcovers and paperbacks. Unable to resist she browsed the titles, a strange mix of crime thrillers, history textbooks, and modern-day romance. She wondered if she would have enough time to borrow one and get lost in a story for a while.

Coming out of the craft room she found Owen in the kitchen, his body bent half-in and half-out of the cupboard under the sink. She paused, admiring the firm curve of his butt and the muscular outline of his back. Then feeling guilty for just standing there, she asked, "Is there anything I can do to help?"

Extracting himself from the cupboard, Owen smiled up at her, "You could do an inventory of the pantry? There should be something we can scrounge up for tonight, but we'll want to do a restock. I've switched the gas on from here, but I'll need to go back out to turn it on from the tank." Rising, he kissed her cheek before leaving out the front door.

Opening the tall pantry cupboard, Caley found that it was stocked with cans of tomatoes, mushrooms, and soup. Clearly labeled plastic containers held pasta, rice, and flour. There were also jars of olives, sauces and a whole shelf of condiments. She was happy to find a canister of coffee and a bowl of sugar, though she doubted there would be milk in the fridge. She hated black coffee, but it would do if she were desperate, definitely better than nothing.

Opening the fridge, she found it as she had expected, empty. The freezer was the same, although the ice cube trays were full. Pulling open the rest of the cupboards she found where the dishes and glasses were stored, everything in its place. Everything was so neat that she felt like an intruder, almost fearful of disturbing anything.

Turning to the lounge room, her gaze was caught by the fireplace. Above it, on the mantel, Caley saw half a dozen framed photographs. Stepping forward to get a closer look, she found herself smiling at the happy faces staring out from them. There was one of Owen, looking to be about the age of five, holding up a salmon larger than he was, his smile so full it showed that three of his top teeth were missing. Another was of him wearing a football jersey, his face covered in game paint. But her favorite was the one of him wearing his police uniform, his beaming mother on one side and his step-father gazing fondly at them both on the other. They looked so happy, so proud, and it made her heart ache a little. Wrapped up in the images she didn't notice Owen's return until he stepped up behind her, wrapping his arms around her waist and gently kissing the back of her neck.

As if reading her mind, he said in a soft voice, "I'm sorry that you never got that with your folks."

Leaning back, pressing her body to his, she sighed. "Dad wanted to take me to a doctor to try and find out what was wrong with me, but my mom was terrified that I would just end up becoming a science experiment. They started fighting all the time, something they'd never really done before I changed. Matthew and Emily couldn't have friends over in case something happened. It was horrible. So, one night, about two weeks after my fifteenth birthday ... I decided I couldn't do this to them anymore ... so I ran. A week later, when I had run out of money and wasn't sure what I should do next, I called my parents. Mom told me not to come home, that some man from the FBI was looking for me, that it wasn't safe. She told me to stay with friends of hers until it was safe to come home. But ... it never was, and I guess I've been running ever since." It was somehow easier to tell Owen the rest of her story when she didn't have to look in his eyes. She knew that he would pity her and she didn't want his pity, it would only make her sad too.

Instead, Owen spun her so that she was facing him and cupped her face in his hands. "You are one of the bravest people I have ever met, putting your family's well-being above your own. I know that there's more and you aren't ready to tell me yet, but I need you to know that you can trust me. I meant it when I said you're not alone anymore." Then bending his head towards her, he kissed her. His lips felt so warm against hers, and she opened her mouth, pressing her body against his, wanting him close.

Their kiss deepened as Owen began to run his hands through her hair and then moved them slowly downwards stroking her neck, then her back. Caley pulled the bottom of Owen's shirt out of his pants and then ran her fingers across the firm skin of his lower back. She felt his gasp against her mouth, surprising her as he bent his legs, his hands taking a firm grip of her buttocks, and in one swift movement lifted her so that she could straddle his waist with her legs. Without breaking their kiss, Owen started to slowly move backward in the direction of the bedroom, his steps hesitant, giving her time to stop this from progressing any further. But the last thing Caley wanted was for this to end, and she ground her hips against him, urging him on.

With one hand Owen held her in place while with the other he fumbled trying to turn the bedroom's doorknob. Getting it open at last, he pushed it wide, carrying her into the room. The windows were open wide and bright noon sunlight streamed in, bathing the room in a golden glow. Turning so that Caley's back was to the bed, Owen gently lowered her on top of the pillows. When he tried to pull back, she took a firmer hold of his neck, drawing him down on top of her, her legs still wrapped around his waist.

It wasn't long, however, before she became frustrated with the barrier of clothes between them. She wanted so badly to feel Owen's skin against hers. Releasing him, she started to undo the top button of his shirt but found, all of a sudden, her hands were trembling so badly she couldn't manage to get it open. Noticing, Owen pulled back even further.

"We don't have to do this, you know?" He asked, his gaze suddenly serious. "We can wait. You don't have to do this so I'll stay. Either way, no matter what, I will protect you. I promise."

If she hadn't already been in love with him, she would have fallen for him at that moment. Never had anyone looked at her the way he was looking at her now. In his eyes, she saw no fear, no disgust, only love, and desire. "I want you Owen, more than I have ever wanted anything. I want you now, I'm tired of missing out, I want to seize this moment right here with you. I'm not trembling because I'm scared, I'm trembling because my body isn't used to feeling like this. Like I'm free."

"Well, alrighty then." Leaning further back, Owen undid the top four buttons of his shirt before pulling it over his head and tossing it to the floor. Then he leaned back down and claimed her mouth with his own, claiming her heart at the same moment.

CHAPTER 16

They made love twice. The first time was hard, fast and passionate, a release of built-up tension and emotion. The second time was slow and loving as inch by inch, they discovered each other's bodies. Learned where each liked to be touched or stroked and giggled because they were ticklish. Now they lay together, the bedclothes thrown back, the late afternoon sun's soft glow glistening through the open window, just gazing at each other. Ignoring the worries of the world in the little bubble of happiness that they had created together.

"I love you, Owen," Caley said shyly, feeling a little foolish to admit something like that to someone she had met little more than a week ago. She could feel the heat rush to her cheeks, waiting for him to brush her off.

"I love you too," he said before kissing her yet again; this time gently on the mouth. Her lips felt slightly bruised from all the kissing they had already done, but that wasn't going to stop her from wanting him to kiss her forever. But after only a few moments, he pulled away.

"I don't want to leave you here alone, but I have to. Mike is going to be wondering where the hell I am, and we are going to have to think of something to tell him. No one knows about the APB except Mike and me, and I think I can convince him to keep it that way, at least until we come up with a way to keep you safe." Her brow furrowed when he mentioned Mike, and he quickly added, "I'm not asking you to tell Mike your secret. You don't have to tell anyone unless you want to. That's your choice. But we have to think of something to tell him."

Reluctantly Caley pulled away from Owen and sat up, resting her back against the pile of pillows pushed up against the headboard. She sighed, a little sad that their bubble had been popped so soon but knowing that Owen was right. They couldn't hide here forever, and they both had responsibilities. She racked her mind, trying to think of a viable story to tell Mike.

"For now, I can just ask him to keep it a secret and maybe invite him to join us for dinner? Give us a chance to come up with a story." Looking at his watch, Owen added, "And I need to get back to work. The Captain will be upset that I haven't checked in. Guess I'm going to have to think of something to explain that too," Owen added with a chuckle. "Not like I can tell him what I've really been doing."

"I've got the day off today, but I'm rostered for the evening shift tomorrow, and I'd hate to let Mel down," Caley admitted.

"Alright. I'm going to leave you my cell phone since

you don't have one of your own and the house phone isn't connected. How about you use it to call her and let her know you won't be back tonight. Once we get this sorted, I don't see any reason why you can't go back to work. But I'd feel much happier if you stayed here instead of at The Last Drop. You're just far too easy to find there if someone comes looking." Caley nodded, a lump forming in her throat at his offer. "If you want, I can stay with you?" Owen asked, hesitantly.

"I'd love that," she said before kissing him.

Caley lay on the bed watching Owen as he got dressed, admiring the view. His uniform was scattered across the bedroom floor, and it took him a while to find everything, especially his belt which had skidded under the bed. For herself, Caley pulled on her sweatshirt and underwear but decided to forgo her jeans. The afternoon was chilly, especially with the breeze coming through open windows, but she still felt warm from their lovemaking. Once Owen left, she would shut the windows, light the wood fire, and have a long soak in the tub, possibly with one of the books.

"Do you think it would be okay if I had a bath?" she asked, suddenly anxious.

Coming over, Owen kissed her on the forehead. "Make yourself at home. Do whatever you want. I'll be back as soon as I can, by dinner time at the latest." Pulling her close, he kissed her, deep and slowly making her blood start to tingle from her lips all the way down to her toes. "I love you, Caley," he murmured, breaking the kiss and quickly hurrying out the door before he could get distracted again. Standing at the open door, watching him get into the police car, she thought how strange life could be and how quickly things could change. That morning she had been ready to run. Now all she wanted to do was stay. Waving until she lost sight of him as he pulled out of the drive, Caley closed the door and with a happy sigh, went to shut the windows.

Owen knew that he should drive straight to the police station, and yet, despite that, he found himself pulling over in front of the Gourmet Basket. He wasn't ready to burst the bubble and let reality come crashing back in. The food store specialized in delicacies from around the world, and Owen couldn't resist the idea of buying a selection of meats, cheese, and fruit for Caley. He also wanted at least one bottle of wine and a bottle of whiskey for Mike. Wandering the aisles, shopping basket in hand, Owen found himself grinning widely at all of the patrons. He couldn't help it unable to remember a time he had felt so happy. While paying for his purchases, the girl operating the checkout noticed his cat-got-the-cream grin and pointed out the bouquets of flowers by the door. Leaving his basket at the register, he went and selected a bunch of red roses mixed with sunflowers.

Leaving the store, Owen realized he must have taken longer shopping than he'd thought. The sun had set, and the full moon glowed brightly with the promise of a beautiful clear night. He shivered as the cold outside air hit him, already imagining laying Caley down on the rug before a roaring fire. When he'd seen couples do that in movies, he had always laughed, but now the idea intrigued him. There were so many firsts that he wanted to experience with Caley. Driving slowly towards the station, trying to delay the inevitable, he practiced how his conversation with Mike was going to go. He hoped like hell that his friend would understand. He just had to find a way to make it so that he had no other option.

Pulling into the station parking lot, he took the time to move the flowers and other purchases from the police car to the passenger seat of his truck. Then, a broad smile still on his face, he headed into the station. But the second he opened the door and caught the look on Mike's face his smile faded. Mike was scowling, and Owen had never seen him look so angry. He was about to open his mouth to say something when Mike came striding towards him and said in a harsh voice, "We need to talk, now!" Without checking back to see if Owen was following Mike stormed off towards the staff room. As soon as he was inside, Mike slammed the door shut before rounding on Owen.

"Where the hell have you been?! Why the hell haven't you been answering your radio?! What the hell is going on?!" Mike demanded.

"It's a long story, but I can explain," Owen said, raising his hands defensively. It had completely slipped his mind that he had turned off his radio after Caley had made her revelation. His cell phone had been switched to silent as he was on duty and, anyway, he'd left it with Caley.

"You better. I've had to cover for you all day. I had to lie to the Captain."

"Caley is somewhere safe. Have you shown the APB to anyone else?"

Mike looked flabbergasted at Owen's question. "No, I haven't, and I've risked my job covering for you. What do you mean Caley is somewhere safe? I don't know what she told you, but she is wanted concerning an armed robbery. She's dangerous, I've been worried like hell all day that something had happened to you."

"What armed robbery?" Owen demanded. "The APB made no mention of a robbery."

"No clue but the guy from the FBI who came in about an hour ago did. I had to lie to the Captain's face and tell him I had no idea about the APB, that it must not have come through for some reason."

"What guy from the FBI?" Owen asked, cold fear running down his spine.

"I don't know, Agent Smithson, I think. Something like that. Does it really matter? I can't remember, I was too busy trying to cover your ass."

"Where is he now?" Owen demanded.

"The captain told him to try The Last Drop," Mike said. "Hey, Owen, are you alright? You've gone pale. I know you like the girl and all, and this had hit you pretty hard but ..."

"I don't like her. I love her, and she's in danger. Whoever that guy is he isn't from the FBI no matter what he says. If he gets his hands on Caley, he'll kill her."

Mike was looking at Owen like he was crazy. "Owen, you need to calm down."

"No what I need to do is get to Caley before anyone else does," Owen said and pushing past Mike he opened the door and sprinted out of the station. He ignored Mike's shout and the sound of the Captain calling out his name, his entire focus was on Caley. Faster than he would have thought possible he was in his car driving towards the house where he had left Caley all alone.

Beside the stack of wood near the fireplace, Caley had discovered a box of kindling, old newspaper, and a matchbox. It hadn't taken her long to start the fire, crouching in front of it while she coaxed the flames to life. Satisfied that it wouldn't go out, Caley wandered into the craft room and spent a happy quarter of an hour browsing the bookshelves. Deciding that her nerves weren't up to handling a thriller, she selected a historical romance. The man on the cover, with his blonde hair and dark brown eyes, reminded her of Owen and it made her smile. Under the sink in the bathroom, she found a collection of scented soaps and bubble bath. Stripping off her sweatshirt and underwear, she sat on the edge of the tub, her feet in basin as she filled the tub. The bubble bath smelled like lavender, and as it wafted through the steam, she felt the tension and stress of the day leave her body. The feel of sliding into the warm water was heavenly, how she'd missed taking warm baths. She vowed to herself that, as long as they were staying in this house, she was going to take a bath every single day.

With her head resting on the edge of the tub, she dried her hands on a nearby towel and picked up the book. She managed to read three chapters before the water temperature dropped too far to be comfortable. Placing the book carefully aside, making sure not to get it wet, she stepped out of the bath. Fluffy white towels hung from the rail, and she took her time drying herself, enjoying the sensation of their softness against her bare skin. Not having a brush, she did her best to comb the tangles out of her hair with her fingers. She was about to pick up her sweatshirt and get dressed when she heard a knock at the door, surprising her. She hadn't thought that Owen would be back so soon. Maybe things hadn't gone well with the Mike. Wrapping the towel around herself, she went to the front door and opened it.

But the man at the door wasn't Owen.

CHAPTER 17

Owen's tires screeched as he pulled out of the station, nearly hitting a pedestrian in his hurry to leave. Pausing only long enough to roll down his window and yell an apology, he slammed his foot on the accelerator. The truck leaped forward, skidding slightly before hurtling forward. Ignoring the speed limit and any rational thoughts about safety, Owen pushed the car to its limits. He would deal with the repercussions once he knew that Caley was safe.

Owen clutched the steering wheel, his knuckles going white. His breathing was ragged, and he tried to get it under control. Owen told himself that she would be fine. He knew that the man was definitely not a member of the FBI. That there was no way the imposter, or anyone else, would ever think to look for Caley at his folks' house. Slowly his nerves steadied, and he released his grip on the wheel, flexing his fingers to relieve the tension. Feeling a little foolish, he relaxed the pressure on the accelerator slowing the car, so it was going only a couple of miles above the speed limit instead of a dozen. As he crested the ridge of the hill, the brightness of the full round moon caught his eye. As a cop, he'd learned that it wasn't merely a superstition that a full moon tended to bring out the crazies. Arrests were always up on that one night a month. Perhaps it was affecting him, letting him imagine the worst. With a calmer mind, he drove on, his thoughts turning to the meal that they would enjoy and the plans they would make to ensure Caley's safety.

The man standing in the doorway was dressed in black pants shirt and jacket with black leather shoes so shined that Caley could see her tense face in their reflection. He was tall, at least a foot taller than Owen, and his head was shaved. His muscles bulged even through his jacket; Caley could make out one vein throbbing at his neck. He looked like he could snap her like a twig if so inclined.

"Hi," Caley said hesitantly unsure what else to say.

"Good evening, ma'am," the man said, "I was wondering if I could have a few moments of your time?"

"Ummm … it's not really a good time," Caley clutched the towel more tightly around her, gesturing to her state of undress with her free hand. "Can you come back later?" she asked, starting to close the door.

"I'm afraid that won't be possible," he said, any facade of pleasantry dropping from his face. Before Caley had a chance to close the door, he had thrust his huge fist against it, causing the wooden door to fly inwards, almost rocking on its hinges.

Turning Caley fled to the bedroom, slamming the door behind her. She searched for a lock only to find there wasn't one. She threw her full weight against it as the ominous man started to pound his fists against the door, making the wood creak.

"Come out, there is nowhere to run. If you don't fight, it will be over quickly, but fight, and I can make you feel pain you never imagined possible."

Desperately Caley searched the room, looking for a weapon or a possible way to escape. But the room held nothing but soft furnishing, even the bedside table lamps were plastic and useless. She cursed herself for having locked the windows. If she hadn't been so security conscious, she could have already escaped and made a run for it. Hidden in the tall grasses until she had time to change form and flee on four paws. Or waited to rip his throat out. But first, she needed to open the window and to do that she needed to buy herself some time.

"You mean like what you did to Hannah?" Caley asked not having to fake the helpless terror in her voice. She felt the man release his pressure on the door. He thought her cornered and it gave him confidence, knowing he only needed to bide his time.

"That little bitch almost broke my arm," he said as if expecting Caley to feel sympathy for him. "Turned her feet into hooves and almost tore the van apart." So Hannah was a horse shifter just like Artemis had said, another part of the dream coming true. "But then the tranquilizer kicked in, and it was all over. I always get them in the end. Could have saved herself a lot of pain if she'd given in to the inevitable." The man was almost bragging now.

"Who do you work for?" Caley asked, slowing moving away from the door. By the dresser was a chair where Owen's mother probably sat to do her makeup. Ten steps that felt like ten miles, and she reached it. Lifting it, she carefully made her way back, angling the chair so that the top of its back rested under the door's handle. It wouldn't hold the man for long, but it was better than nothing.

"Beats me. But as long they keep paying me nicely, I'll keep bringing in girls like you. They told me that you can turn into a dog so I can't see you giving me much trouble. Now be a good little bitch and come out." The man let out a couple of woofing noises and then she heard laughter. She wished she was in wolf form now so she could slash that smile off his face. But to shift, she needed a clear mind, and that was unlikely now.

Stepping slowly, her feet gliding just above the carpeted floor, she headed towards the window. "How did you find me?" she asked.

"When the Captain at the station mentioned you and one of his officers were friendly I asked for the guy's number which he provided. When the woman at the bar said you were out with him, I used my contacts to track his phone. I thought I was going to have to kill him too, but I guess I just got lucky," He chuckled. "Now stop your stalling and open the door. I'll give you to the count of five. One ... Two."

Caley knew that she was out of time, and she was still three paces away from the window. With no other option, she sprinted to the window, fumbling with the lock as her wildly beating heart pumped her fear through her body, making her hands go clammy.

"Okay, I'm coming out," she shouted, trying to buy herself a few more minutes. But something in her tone must have alerted her attacker that something wasn't quite right because she heard a rattle as he tried to turn the door handle. Since there was no lock, the handle turned, but as he tried to push the door open, it caught on the chair.

"What the fuck?" he exclaimed. Caley heard a crunch as the man started to throw his considerable weight against the door. The wooden door seemed to curve inwards on its frame from the impact of his body crashing against it, and the chair creaked. It wouldn't hold for long.

With a desperate shove, Caley managed to release the window's lock. Pushing the window open, she swung one leg and then the other over the ledge. For a second, her towel caught in the window's lock, but with a hard tug, Caley managed to pull it free. She wished she had time to grab her clothes, feeling so exposed and vulnerable wearing only a towel, but that would take minutes she couldn't afford to spare. Once Caley shifted, it would no longer matter, she just had to find a place where she could hide for five minutes to change her form. Looking around, the light from the full moon bathing the area in an eerie white glow, she tried to figure out where to hide. The shed was locked and anyway too obvious. There were trees which acted as a barrier along the front fence line of the property, but in a single line, they wouldn't provide much cover.

Her best bet were the long grasses covering the front yard of the property. Sprinting across the gravel driveway, Caley felt pain shoot across her bare feet as sharp stones shredded the tender flesh of her soles. She grimaced, biting back a scream. Caley had only barely managed to make it ten feet into the grass when the splintering sound of the bedroom door being smashed apart reached her. Instantly she dropped to the ground, curling up into a ball, trying to be as small as she could. Her heart pounded loudly in her ears. Closing her eyes, she attempted to pull her magic from her core into her body, but it didn't work. She couldn't focus on the image of a wolf in her mind, not with the man swearing behind her as he climbed through the window and then the crunch of his boots as he crossed the gravel drive.

"Got you now, you little bitch!" he screamed as he caught sight of her. Unable to defend herself, she felt him grab her, her towel falling away as he slung her roughly over his broad shoulder. She pounded his back with her fists, kicking her legs, trying to get him to loosen his grip to no avail. It was like he was made of steel for all the reaction her struggle incited. Reaching the front door, he didn't bother to turn the handle, instead with one hard kick of his booted foot he smashed it inwards. When he reached the middle of the living room, he dropped her, head first, onto the floor. Her head hit the ground with a thump, barely missing the wooden coffee table. The impact made her head spin, and for a moment, her vision went black as her body threatened to fade into unconsciousness. But she fought the urge, knowing if she blacked out that would be the end.

"You could have made this easy on yourself, but no, you decided to fight. What comes next is on you," the man moved to the table and picked up one of the two chairs dragging it back to the living room. Picking Caley up from the floor, his grip so hard it would leave bruises, he thrust her into the chair. When he turned his back, she tried to run, but still dizzy from the impact of her earlier fall, he stopped her before she made it two paces. Catching her, he pushed her back into the chair and then pulling back his arm he punched her in the face. His fist collided with her cheek so hard that her head whipped to the side. Blood filled her mouth as she bit her cheek, and she swore she heard the bone crack. She barely had time to register the pain before he smashed his fist into the other side of her face, and her head was flung in the other direction.

Panic didn't hit Owen again until he turned into his parents' road and, sighting their house, he glimpsed the dark sedan parked in the driveway. Then sudden panic hit him like a lightning bolt - straight to the heart. His first instinct was to hit the accelerator, but something made him pause. Instead of speeding up, he slowed the car and dimmed the headlights. Whoever was in the house with Caley wasn't going to be someone friendly, and he didn't want to risk startling them. The crunch of the gravel driveway under the truck's tires made him wince, seeming to echo across the open yard but he could discern no reaction from inside the house. The lights were on, but he could make nothing out through the drawn curtains. Pulling his truck up next to the unknown vehicle, he parked so that it would be partially shielded from view.

Turning off the truck's interior light so it wouldn't alert anyone he leaned over to the passenger side and opened the glove box. He pulled out his spare Glock, already loaded with six rounds, and the pair of handcuffs. Slowly he opened his car door and stepped out. Unclicking the safety on the gun he moved to the sedan, placing his feet carefully so as not to make a sound. The element of surprise could be his only advantage. The car's windows were darkly tinted, but the rental company's logo was proudly displayed on the windshield. On the passenger seat, he made out an open manila folder. Squinting, he managed to just make out Caley's photo, the same one from the APB, paper clipped to the top.

Wondering if perhaps he should have called for backup his thoughts were shattered when he heard a sound that made his blood run cold. Caley had begun to scream.

CHAPTER 18

Gun held out in front of him, finger hovering over the trigger, Owen sprinted to the front door. With one hard kick, the door swung open. During his time in the police force, Owen had visited several crime scenes. A handful of them had been the result of violent actions. But Peregrine City was a quiet town, and nothing in his past had prepared him to what he saw as he entered his parents' house. In the middle of the living room, Caley sat, unconscious, tied to one of the dining room chairs. She was naked, but it took his brain a moment to register this fact, as her body was almost completely covered in blood and bruises so that only a few patches of undamaged skin showed through. Her head was slumped to one side, face swollen and bruised so badly that he barely recognized her. Blood dripped from dozens of wounds, pooling on the rug and likely staining the floor beneath.

The sound of the door being smashed open roused the man who had been kneeling between Caley's parted legs.

The man was shirtless, probably having removed it to prevent it from being covered in blood, but the sight of it made Owen's blood curdle with rage. Boosting himself to a standing position, the man looked at Owen in a derogatory way.

"The boyfriend, I presume?" he sniggered.

"Caley are you alright?" Owen asked but got no response. "Caley?" he tried again.

"Oh, she's in no fit state to hold a conversation I'm afraid. Put up quite a fight. But I did warn her that I'd make it hard on her if she fought me," the attacker answered in a tone so matter of fact it was like he was talking to Owen about the state of the economy. He was also edging slowly backward. Looking behind him, Owen spotted what he was going for. A gun, still in its holster, lay on the kitchen bench. Five more steps and he would reach it.

Pointing his own gun so that it was aimed to fire directly into the middle of the man's forehead, Owen warned, "Stop right there. You're under arrest."

The man stopped, but instead of looking worried, he laughed. "You can't arrest me. You have no authority over me. You have no idea who you are dealing with."

"I know that you're not FBI and I'm also pretty sure that you murdered Hannah and a string of other girls," Owen said.

"I'd show you my badge, but it's in my jacket pocket," he said, gesturing to where his black jacket hung on the back of the couch, his black shirt folded neatly over it. Nothing about this man implied that he was erratic, everything indicated how pre-meditated his actions were.

How much joy he seemed to take in each small step. One part of Owen's mind came to these conclusions as the other part watched the assailant make a move towards the jacket.

"I said, stop. Now! I want you to step to your right. Move away from Caley," Owen commanded.

The man's eyes flickered towards Caley's still form. "Don't think you can save her. That draining tube is inserted directly into her femoral artery. I would say she has less than three minutes before she bleeds out."

Owen wanted desperately to go to Caley, he needed to stop the bleeding. But doing so would play right into his opponent's hands. With hands as steady as stone, he kept his gun pointed at the man's forehead. "Put your hands up where I can see them and take two steps backward." The man hesitated for a moment and then, drawing the moment out, slid first one foot and then the other taking two slow steps back. His hands, open palms out, were raised to his waistline and no further.

"Put your hands up higher," Owen said, trying to keep the frustration at the man's stalling out of his voice. But from the way the man's thin lips twisted to one side, he could sense his pleasure in the stalling, that he was enjoying making Owen's blood boil.

A groan from Caley caught Owen's attention, reassuring him that she was still alive. That there was still hope. Unable to resist the urge, his eyes flickered in her direction, craving the visual reassurance, and he took a hesitant step towards her. It was all the invitation that the man needed. In five lunging paces, he was in the kitchen grabbing his gun from its holster. In the time it took for

Owen to realize his mistake, the man had aimed the gun at him. Pointing his own gun once again at the assailant Owen groaned realizing that they were at a stalemate. All the man had to do was prevent Owen from staunching Caley's bleeding for a few more minutes, and he would lose her forever.

"Drop the gun," Owen ordered, trying to keep the fear out of his voice. But the man only laughed.

"You first buddy," he said, mouth curving into a cruel smile.

Again, Caley groaned. Somehow, despite her horrible wounds, she was still fighting, this time to regain consciousness. He heard the chair legs scrape against the floor. He couldn't afford to turn his head to check but guessed that she was starting to struggle against her bonds.

"Silly girl," the man crooned "Doesn't she realize that struggling isn't going to help her? It will just increase her blood flow."

"Owen."

He heard his name, so soft it was barely audible, but the sound made everything around him seem too still. Later, much later, Owen would look back on the next few moments in wonder. In his frantic mind, those seconds seemed to last an eon. He had never shot anyone; he had never had the need. His mother had raised him to value life above all else. But the clarity of truth had come over him. That this night was going to end in only one of two ways. With Caley or the man in black dead and it was up to him to choose which of the two it would be. And he knew that no matter what it would cost him, there was only one choice he could make. For a brief moment, he considered merely wounding the man but quickly pushed the thought aside. The man could be given no opportunity to retaliate. Taking a deep breath, Owen aimed his gun at the center of the man's forward and pulled the trigger.

CHAPTER 19

Before the attacker's body had even hit the floor, Owen was at Caley's side. Being this close to her, the damage inflicted was even more horrific. His hand trembled slightly, fearful of doing more harm than good, not knowing where to start. He had to resist the urge to undo her restraints, seeing her helpless and bound he wanted nothing more than to grant her freedom. But, before anything else, he needed to remove the needle which continued to pump her life out her femoral artery.

Kneeling in front of her, blood quickly soaking through his pants, he looked at the needle's insertion point. The large silver needle penetrated the smooth skin of her inner right thigh. Deep red blood moved up the attached tube, filling a bag plumped to almost full. He was tempted to rip it out, but if any air managed to hit Caley's bloodstream, there would be nothing he could do to save her. Placing one hand below the needle to hold the limb in place he prepared to remove it, wincing as even the slight movement elicited another moan from Caley. Her entire thigh was a blur of bruises. With his other hand, he slowly drew the needle out. As the sharp point exited, blood started to gush from the wound.

"Shit," Owen exclaimed, quickly using both hands to apply firm pressure to the wound. His eyes scanned the room, looking for anything he could use as a bandage and spotted the folded black shirt. Maintaining pressure on the wound with one hand, Owen leaned towards the chair, stretching out his fingers to clasp the shirt. Biting the hem, he tore a strip off the shirt. One piece was all he could afford to use knowing that Caley would have other injuries which would need binding before he could even think about moving her. Removing his hand only long enough to slide in the cloth, he quickly reapplied the pressure. Another tear of the shirt and he had a strip long enough to wrap around Caley's thigh.

"I'm so sorry, Caley, but this is going to hurt," Owen muttered, not sure if she could hear him but needing it to say it anyway. Placing one hand under her leg, he lifted it. Instead of a groan, the movement made Caley scream, the pain rousing her out of her unconscious state. Instantly she started to struggle against her bonds, forcing Owen to grip her leg even harder.

"Caley, stop. It's Owen. I'm trying to save you," he pleaded. His voice seemed to calm the struggling girl, and she stilled, her scream faltering into a sob.

"Owen?" she gasped.

"I'm here, sweetheart. But we need to get you some help, and it needs to happen fast. I'm going to try my best not to hurt you too much, but I also don't want to lie to you. You're cut up pretty bad and if I don't get you to a hospital -"

Caley cut him off. "No hospitals. They can't find out what I am."

"But Caley I don't know how to help you. How about a doctor?"

"No doctors."

"A vet?" he asked, only half-joking. When she didn't respond, he thought at first that she had been insulted by the question. But looking up he realized that she slipped back into unconsciousness again. It was probably for the best. Hopefully, it would save her from experiencing the pain he knew he was going to inflict by dealing with the injuries. Lifting her leg, once again he used the strip of the shirt to secure the pressure bandage he had created in place. With both hands now free, he sprinted to the kitchen, opening the drawers until he found a knife which would suit his purposes. He sawed through the plastic ties which bound Caley to the chair, managing to only just catch her before she fell. Lifting her gingerly into his arms, he carried her, still naked and bleeding, to the truck.

It took some effort, but he managed to get the back door open without letting go of Caley's limp body. Not caring if he got blood on his once-prized upholstery, he lifted her and slid her as gently as he could manage across the back seat. She let out a moan as her bare, wounded skin touched the scratchy material but apart from that uttered no sound. Rummaging under the passenger seat, he grabbed the folded wool blanket and shook it open. As gently as he could, he laid it over Caley. It didn't seem right somehow to leave her naked and exposed even if there was no one there to see. She was vulnerable enough as it was, and he wanted to do everything he could to save her from any further trauma. Pulling his keys out of his pocket, he got into the driver's seat and thrust them into the ignition. He was about to start the engine when he faltered. He had no idea what his next move was.

Caley didn't want to go to a hospital or a doctor, and he felt that he should honor her wishes. For a minute, he even considered a vet, but in this form, a vet would laugh them straight out of his premises. Looking at her, he wondered if she could shift but quickly dismissed the idea. His own first aid training was basic. What he needed was someone who had medical training, someone he could trust.

Picking up his phone, he dialed Mike's cell number. Mike picked up on the third ring.

"Owen, what the fucking hell is going on?" Mike demanded, clearly upset.

"I promise I'll tell you everything. But first, I need you to meet me at Lisa's."

Owen drove 20 miles over the speed limit all the way from his parents' house to Lisa's place, which was on the other side of town. He cringed every time he hit a bump or when the truck swayed as he flew around a corner knowing that the rocky journey would be torture on Caley's injured body. But the idea of her bleeding out before Owen reached help made him push the car to its limits. He only hoped that Lisa's training as a dental nurse would be enough to save Caley.

Mike and Lisa were both sitting on the steps of Lisa's porch, waiting for them as Owen pulled the car into a screeching stop against the curb. Getting out of the vehicle, Owen shouted, "Help me," to Mike who came racing to meet him as he opened the rear door of the truck. Taking in the sight of Caley, Mike's eyes went wide with shock, but he managed to bite back any questions. Instead, Mike slid his hands under Caley's shoulders, carefully sliding her towards him until Owen was able to lift her and cradle her against his chest.

"Lisa, open the door," Mike instructed. As Lisa ran to do as bid, Owen carried Caley towards the house. Mike held back, scanning the road for any sign that they had been followed. The FBI agent had not seemed the type to give up his quarry without a fight. Seeing no sign of him Mike followed Owen into the house, wondering what the hell his friend had gotten himself into.

Owen, cradling Caley in his arms, followed Lisa down the hallway, turning left into her living room. He had only been there once when he had shared an awkward dinner with her and Mike. He had hated always being the third wheel, and found dinner at Lisa's house was just too intimate to be comfortable.

"I'll grab some blankets, give me a sec," Lisa said, running to the linen closet. She came back within moments holding two striped cotton blankets. The first Lisa laid over the long end of her modular couch. Owen guessed it must be new, he didn't remember it from his last visit, and his good opinion of Lisa increased when she seemed to not care if Caley dripped blood on it. He silently promised to buy her a new one when this was all over.

"Are you sure you shouldn't take her to the hospital?" Lisa asked, her eyes widening as she took in the extent of Caley's injuries.

"I promised her I wouldn't."

"Alright but just remember that I'm not a doctor. I'm just a dental hygienist. I don't know how much I can do."

Owen nodded, he knew the risks. Sighing, Lisa left the room to fetch her medical kit. Owen knelt down next to the couch and slowly stroked Caley's hair. In her unconscious state, she looked years younger, so innocent.

"Owen, what the hell is going on? You aren't just risking your own job now, you are risking mine and Lisa's. We have the right to know what we are risking them for."

Turning his head to look up at his friend Owen tried to swallow the lump that was forming in his throat. What could he possibly say that would make Mike believe him? He just hoped that all their years of friendship, of working together, would be enough that Mike wouldn't throw him out of the house.

CHAPTER 20

Telling Mike and Lisa that Caley could change into a dog or wolf had gone pretty much as Owen had expected. He watched his friends' emotions change from shock to awkward amusement, to outrage. Mike yelled at him to stop playing games and then asked if he was on some kind of hallucinogenic drugs. The worst part of it all was that Owen couldn't even blame them for their reactions. If Caley hadn't changed form in his car, his response would likely have been identical to theirs. He wished he had time to take a polygraph test or at least a drug test but looking at Caley lying weak, barely breathing on Lisa's couch he knew that wasn't an option.

While Owen argued with Mike, Lisa swabbed Caley's wounds with disinfectant and bandaged up what she could with the basic tools she had on hand. Many of cuts needed stitches which were far outside of Lisa's realm of expertise. She guessed that most of the bruises would heal given time, but she was worried about an almost black one which spread across Caley's abdomen. It looked like she could have internal bleeding, but again Lisa was only guessing. Deep wounds and internal bleeding weren't really something you came across when working in a dental practice. Lisa didn't know what to think about Owen's revelations. Mike clearly felt that his friend was crazy, but Lisa wasn't so sure. When she couldn't sleep, she had developed the habit of watching late-night documentaries on strange occurrences. If she could believe that alien abductions might be real, then maybe she could believe this. Maybe.

Standing up, planning to go to the kitchen and get a glass of water to drip-feed Caley, Lisa suddenly froze. Her mouth went dry, and blood rushed to her head so fast she thought that she was going to faint. "Guys," Lisa said, or tried to, her mouth so dry she could barely get the word out. She swallowed, running her tongue around her mouth before trying again. "Hey, guys." The words came out fine, but Owen and Mike were arguing so loudly that neither man heard her. Frustrated, she tried a third time, raising her voice almost to a shout, "Guys!"

"What is it, babe?" Mike said, only half turning towards her, his glaring gaze still focused on Owen.

"Ummm … I think you should see this. Owen was right." This time her words caught the attention of both men though their reactions were quite different. Mike looked towards the couch and at the sight of the reddish-brown wolf laying in Caley's place his knees began to give way, making him stagger and grab the back of the couch for support. Owen, on the other hand, rushed to the front of the sofa and knelt beside the wolf's head. With no concern for his fingers, he began to softly stroke its muzzle.

As Caley floated towards consciousness, she became aware of voices murmuring somewhere behind her. Her body tensed, ready to flee, but then she recognized Owen's warm voice and her body instantly relaxed. Caley felt stiff and sore. She tried to open her eyes, but the bright light was blindingly painful, and she closed them tight against the pain. Flexing her hands and feet, she was relieved to feel soreness instead of sharp pain. Hopefully, that meant that nothing was broken. But as she started to stretch out her legs, panic swept through her. For as she had stretched out her leg, it had released something she hadn't been expecting. Her tail.

The shock acted as a catalyst and without having to think Caley transformed. She had never changed so fast before, never even known that it was possible. Perhaps it shouldn't have been because the reshaping of her bones, the tearing, and stretching of her muscles, the process of morphing from a wolf into woman caused bolts of agony to shoot through her entire being. Unable to prevent herself, she cried out.

Within seconds Owen was at her side. "Caley, are you alright? What's wrong?"

She almost wanted to laugh at his question. What was wrong? More like what was right? Only she was pretty sure that laughing would hurt her tender ribs. "Where am I?"

"You're at Lisa's house. I didn't know where else to take you. But you're safe now. He can't hurt you anymore. And I trust Mike and Lisa."

Caley lifted her head slightly, turning to see Lisa and Mike standing a little distance away behind the couch. Lisa gave her a shy smile, but Mike wouldn't meet her eyes, and she felt her feeling of ease dissipate. He must think her some kind of freak. Dropping her head in shame, she was horrified to see that she had clawed two sets of large tears into Lisa's couch.

"Lisa, I am so sorry. I didn't mean too. I'll find some way to pay you back," Caley promised.

"Don't worry about it. Anyway, Owen has already offered to buy me a replacement. If you are feeling up to it, I have some clothes you might want to borrow?"

Caley's mouth dropped open as she turned her gaze on her stark naked body. She was so used to changing fully clothed that it had never occurred to her that she wouldn't be dressed.

"Here," Owen said a little sheepishly holding out a blanket and draping it over her.

As Caley wrapped it around herself, Lisa gasped, startling her. Looking in her direction, Caley saw that the brunette girl's eyes were wide as saucers. Caley thought it was fear until Lisa said in a voice full of awe, "You're almost healed. When Owen carried you in here, I thought the chances of you pulling through were slim. You looked like you had internal bleeding and several gashes were really nasty. But I can hardly make out the bruise on your abdomen anymore. Plus most of the wounds seemed to have healed."

"Did changing form make you heal faster? Is that why you did it?" Mike asked, this time looking Caley straight in the eye. There was no animosity in his question, only wonder.

"I don't know, maybe. I've never been badly injured like this before. But I didn't shift form on purpose. It sometimes happens when I sleep, maybe my subconscious just took over."

"Well, either way, I'm grateful you are on the mend," Owen said, leaning over and kissing her brow. "It will definitely make our plans easier."

"What plans?" Caley asked.

Caley sat with the others at Lisa's dining table, a mug of tea warming her hands. She had borrowed a loose pullover and a pair of tracksuit pants from Lisa. Spread across the table lay an assortment of maps on which Mike and Owen had marked each spot where a girl had gone missing.

"The only way you are ever going to be able to stop running is if we find out who is behind all this," Owen explained. "By looking at the killer's pattern, we might be able to determine where he came from."

"You don't buy his story about being FBI?" Caley asked, taking a sip of her tea.

"His badge looked real enough, but there was something off about him. It's a shame that I didn't get a closer look at his ID, I could have run it through the central database," said Mike.

"His ID is probably still in his jacket, which is still where he left it in my parents' place. With his body," Owen said.

"It was self-defense," Caley responded, instantly addressing Owen's unspoken thoughts.

"You know that, and I know that, but it will be our word against whoever is paying his wages. I doubt you want to take the stand and I have the feeling that whoever that guy was working for they are far more influential than a small city cop," Owen explained.

"So, what do I do?" Caley asked, gripping the cup hard to try and hide that fact that her hands had started to tremble. She had thought her life of running was over. Now it appeared she would have to run even faster.

"No I, not anymore, it's we," Owen said, looking her straight in the eye. "I told you, you don't have to do this alone anymore." He reached across the table and took her hand, giving it a reassuring squeeze. She returned the pressure with a grateful smile, not quite able to believe that this wonderful man was willing to give up a mundane life for her. "The plan," Owen continued, "Is that we retrace the killer's route. Find out if he left any clues, talk to people who knew the murdered girls, try to find anything that points us to the money trail. Find the money we'll find whoever is behind this."

"While you're gone, I'll do some digging of my own, and I'll try and delay them discovering the body for as long as I can," Mike offered. "We'll need to think of a cover story for your absence."

"Stress leave for having my girlfriend go missing?" Owen asked.

Before Mike could respond, Caley interrupted them. "We can't follow the killer's trail. We have to go to New York."

Owen looked puzzled, "What's in New York?"

"Felix. He's the guy who does my fake IDs, and you are going to need one. But more than that, Felix is an amazing hacker. If anyone can find my sisters, he can."

"Sisters?" Owen looked even more confused than before. "I thought you only had one sister. Emily?"

"I only have one blood sister, that's true. But there are other shifters like me, and they are also being hunted. I need to find them and warn them before it's too late."

"How do you know all this?" Mike asked.

"Well, it's a good thing you guys are all sitting down because my story is about to get even stranger."

CHAPTER 21

Caley licked the lip of the envelope and sealed it. Picking up a pen, she wrote Melody's name on the outside. Lisa had promised to deliver it to The Last Drop in a couple of weeks, once everyone had stopped looking for her. Caley hadn't been able to tell Mel everything, nothing that would make it possible for anyone to trace them, but she had at least taken the chance to say thank you and goodbye. Caley laid the envelope on top of the two postcards. One was to her family, letting them know she was safe and moving on. The other was addressed to a post office box in New York. Like the one to her family, it bore no signature.

"Looking forward to watching Season 3 Episode 6 of True Blood with you. I'll bring the popcorn and drinks."

Felix loved binge-watching television shows, and True

Blood was his code for Caley. Something about how the red-haired vamp Jessica reminded him of her. How shocked he would be to find out she was more werewolf than a vampire. The season and episode numbers would set the time, 36 hours from the date on the postcard. Popcorn and drinks placed the order for passport and driver's license. They would mail the cards as they left and hope that this one would reach Felix before they did.

Her only job done, Caley wandered aimlessly around the house. Despite her protests, the others decided that it wasn't safe for her to leave the house, not with the APB out and the cops looking for her. Not until they were ready to leave. So, while she waited here patiently, her friends put themselves at risk to help her. Mike had gone to the station to spread the rumor about Owen going off the rails and needing some time alone. Lisa had gone to work to try and raid extra medical supplies without being seen. Once she had those, Lisa was going shopping to buy extra clothes, and toiletries for Caley since going back to the tavern wasn't an option. Caley was heart-broken at the idea of losing the photograph of her family. Leaving the arrowhead behind was also a concern. But Lisa had promised to collect her things and send them on for her. So, in the end, she had no choice but to be content with that.

Owen had driven to a town three counties over to trade in his car for the cash they would need to pay for their new IDs and fund their escape. He would also withdraw all the money from his accounts before anyone had the chance to freeze them. Before he'd left, he'd checked the car sales sites on Lisa's computer and made arrangements to check out a few. Nothing fancy or which would attract unwanted attention, just a set of wheels to get them to New York. Until they spoke to Felix, Caley had no idea where to even begin looking for the other huntresses. For all she knew they could be spread across the United States or even the world.

Lisa was the first to arrive home, her hands full of Wal-Mart bags. Together the two women removed all the tags and folded the clothes, putting them into the duffel bag which Lisa had also purchased. Once done they sat together on the couch and Lisa flicked on the television to an episode of Family Feud. Neither really paid the show much attention, their thoughts on other things, but the background noise gave a sense of comfort and normality. Both jumped when they heard a loud knock on the door and were relieved to spot Mike through the window.

Caley was starting to worry as the clock reached 7pm with still no sign of Owen. What if he had been pulled over? What if he had changed his mind? Sensing her unease, Mike offered her a beer to calm her nerves. She was about to accept when she saw a pair of headlights turn into the road and then a brown Ford pull up out front. Unable to stop herself, Caley threw caution to the wind and rushed to the front door. Opening it, she hurtled down the stairs and threw herself into Owen's waiting arms. For a long moment, they just stood there, each reassuring themselves of the other's safety.

At a much more sedate pace, Mike and Lisa joined them. "Can I give you a hand bringing anything in?" Mike offered.

Their original plan had been to wait until morning to

leave so Caley was surprised when Owen said, "No thanks. I actually thought it might be best if we head off now. Drive for a few hours and then find a motel somewhere for the night. Fewer witnesses and you two have risked enough."

Mike's eye crinkled with disappointment, but he nodded. Caley headed back into the house to grab the duffel bag, giving the friends time to say their goodbyes. She stalled for a while, and when she headed back out the front door, Mike and Owen were breaking from an embrace. Caley hugged Lisa, thanking her for everything, and then offered her hand to Mike. But instead of shaking it, he pulled her into a hug. "You take care of my friend," he whispered in her ear. She nodded, afraid that if she tried to say anything, she would cry.

Always the gentleman, Owen opened the passenger door for her. The Ford wasn't as fancy inside as Owen's truck had been and it smelled slightly of stale cigarettes, but none of that mattered. It would take them to New York, and that was what was necessary. Waving a final goodbye to their friends, Owen drove the car away.

They drove in silence for twenty minutes, both lost in their own thoughts. Caley mind raced trying to figure out a plan, to work out what to do next to complete her quest, an idea that didn't seem so strange, nor so funny anymore. She was nervous, scared that she would let the others down, that she would let Artemis down. But most of all, she was grateful. Grateful that no matter what happened next, she wouldn't have to face it alone.

AFTERWORD

Want to know what happens to Caley and Owen in New York City? You can continue the journey with us in Book 2 of the "Gifts From the Goddess" series, "Hunter's Pride"; due for release early 2020.

We can't wait to introduce you to Portia, our sexy feline shifter, and the first of Caley's huntress sisters. When canine meets feline, what could possibly go wrong?

Head to www.mirandaharvey.com or www.catealexander-author.com to find our other books and to find how to connect with us, so you don't miss all the updates on "Hunter's Pride."

Until next time, happy reading.

Miranda and Cate xx

PS Keep reading for a sneak peek in to "Hunter's Pride."

ACKNOWLEDGMENTS

Behind every author, there is a team of people who helped bring the story to life.

Firstly we would like to thank our fabulous writing group, the Knovel Knights, without who we would never have met and started this journey. Their support, encouragement, and desserts made this book a possibility. Special thanks go to Rebekah Prince who helped two Aussies use correct American lingo.

Secondly, thank you to all the amazing authors from the Fated Mates Boxed Set. We are so grateful to have met you and know we have made friends for life. A special thank you to April Canavan, our fearless box set leader, for keeping us on track and making us laugh so hard it hurt.

To our editors and proofreaders, Ash Spring, Josie Cudmore, and Ruth Fawcett thank you. You found, hopefully, all the remaining typos which snuck through all the drafts in the first edition. You add the polish we would lack without out you and any remaining mistakes are entirely our own fault.

Our beautiful cover was designed by Amala at Mayflower studios who brings to life the images we have in our head.

Finally, thank you to everyone who has bought, shared, and reviewed "Wolf Moon." We hope you loved it.

Miranda and Cate

PS Sometimes working with another person on a project can be hard, but working with Cate has been a dream and so much fun. She is my word twin, my cheer-leader and I could not have done this without her. Go team Miracat - Miranda.

PPS I need to thank Miranda for asking me to co-author this book with her. I had no idea what I was getting into when we joined the Fated Mates Box Set, but I'm so glad she did! And, lastly, thank you to my daughters, Reanna, Erin and Aimee, for all their love and support, and their patience while I'm buried in imaginary worlds. My darlings, I might have dedicated the book to Alice, but everything I do, I do for you. Cate (aka Mama) x

ABOUT MIRANDA HARVEY

By day Miranda battles numbers and spreadsheets. At night she adventures into fantasy worlds of her own imagination using her powers as a wordsmith to bring her characters to life. She lives in Western Australia with her husband and two dogs, Bronson and Kira, who can often be found wandering the pages of her books.

Her first book in the Rift Magic series, Guardians of Wundor, was published on her birthday in 2018. To find out more and to become a Rifter, go to www.mirandaharvey.com

ABOUT CATE ALEXANDER

A teen mum turned lawyer, with an undergraduate degree in history, Cate's daughters suddenly grew so she decided she actually had time to fulfil her life-long plan of becoming an author. She now spends her nights creating magical worlds, finding magic in everyday reality, and then putting it all into words so she can share her stories with other people.

To find out more about Cate, including how to connect with her on social media, go to www.catealexanderauthor.com

HUNTER'S PRIDE

Prologue

C*uckoo! Cuckoo! Cuckoo! Cuckoo! Cuckoo! Cuckoo!*
Portia popped open the bottle of Moet just as the clock struck six.

Pouring the champagne into a crystal flute, she could almost hear her grandmother's Southern voice reminding her that a lady doesn't drink before five.

"Here's to you, Grandma," Portia smiled, lifting the glass, as she toasted the cuckoo clock and the matriarch's memory. Her New York penthouse was mostly furnished in sleek modern furniture. She wanted the décor to highlight the artwork on her walls, not overwhelm it, but some pieces of family history had to stay. She would never give up her Grandma's cuckoo clock, or the patchwork quilt folded neatly at the end of her bed. Friends and business acquaintances thought they were ironic statements on the rare occasions Portia opened up her home, but to Portia, they were visual reminders to stay grounded.

At precisely five minutes past six, Portia's phone lit up. She moved quickly to her laptop, opening so the screen faced inwards into the apartment so she could curl up in an easy chair rather than sitting at her desk.

"Hey, Mom, Pop!" she said, raising her glass to her parents, "Happy Tuesday."

"Happy Tuesday to you too, darling girl," her mother raised her own champagne glass, while her father took the first sip of his whiskey.

Routine was important. Rituals and routines. As an only child, Portia's parents had always encouraged her to be independent.

The only person you can rely on is yourself.

You're responsible for your own actions, my girl.

You can do anything, but only you can get you there.

But at the same time, they'd also taught her that family was the most important thing and, as such, it didn't matter how busy and successful you were, you always made time for family. Her parents had lived these lessons and, now she was busy living her own life, Portia had a new appreciation for scheduling time for those who matter to you.

Sipping champagne in the comfort of her own home, catching up on all the news with her parents, was a treasured hour in her week and one that was very rarely missed. One of her favorite times of the week. Until it got to the bit about Portia's love life.

"So darling," her Mom began, "Have you seen that

lovely boy again. Jeremy, was it? It sounded like you've had a few fun dates."

"No," Portia cut her mother off, even knowing how much her mother hated one-word responses.

Her mother raised one elegant eyebrow. "Now, Portia."

"Honey," it was her dad's turn to interrupt, "Portia is a busy young woman. No need to worry about her. She's got her mother's looks. She'll find a man when she wants one." Both women gave him identical glares, dark eyes daring him to keep going. "Ok," he raised his hands in defeat, "I know when my attentions aren't wanted."

"No, Mom," Portia gave in, "I am not seeing Jeremy again. He wasn't right for me. I thought he was a nice guy, but I think he was just looking for a black woman to shock his family."

"So last century," her Mom was back on her side, "I thought we were way past this. But Pop is right about one thing. You are too pretty to stay single for long. Just make sure you include time for love in that busy schedule of yours. You're my favorite accomplishment, and I want you to be happy."

"Love you, Mom, Pop, but I do need to go. Early start tomorrow." Blowing kisses at the computer screen, Portia logged off.

She felt a bit guilty being so blunt with her parents, but she was a 24-year-old woman. Her love life, or lack thereof, was her business. No one else's, not even well-meaning parents. Her Mom had made her own choices, and her regrets about leaving motherhood too late, and only having one child was not Portia's issue.

Ugh. Now Portia was all worked up again. Time for

dinner, followed by a long, hot shower to calm her nerves. She could feel herself twitching, and that was one sensation she didn't like.

Twenty minutes later, Portia stepped out of the shower. She hadn't been joking about an early night. It was only 7pm, yet she felt well and truly ready for bed. Drying herself off, Portia didn't even bother with a robe, walking lightly through her room and throwing herself onto the bed. By the time she landed, she had shifted into the form of a sleek black cat. Some people thought of cats as being nocturnal, but for Portia, it was the best way to get a solid night's sleep. Just as soon as her damn tail stopped twitching.